ACCLAIM FOR THE NOVELS OF OPAL CAREW

"A blazing hot erotic romp . . . A must-read for lovers of erotic romance. A fabulously fun and stupendously steamy read for a cold winter's night. This one's so hot, you might need to wear oven mitts while you're reading it!" —*Romance Junkies*

4 stars! "Carew's devilish twists and turns keep the emotional pitch of the story moving from sad to suspenseful to sizzling to downright surprising in the end. . . . The plot moves swiftly and satisfyingly." —*Romantic Times BOOKreviews*

"Fresh, exciting, and extremely sexual, with characters you'll fall in love with. Absolutely fantastic!" —*Fresh Fiction*

"The constant and imaginative sexual situations along with likable characters with emotional depth keep the reader's interest. Be prepared for all manner of coupling, including groups, exhibitionism, voyeurism, and same-sex unions. . . . I recommend *Swing* for the adventuresome who don't mind singeing their senses." —*Regency Reader*

"Carew pulls off another scorcher. . . . She knows how to write a love scene that takes her reader to dizzying heights of pleasure." —*My Romance Story*

"So much fun to read . . . The story line is fast-paced, with wonderful humor." —*Genre Go Round Reviews*

"A great book . . . Ms. Carew has wonderful imagination." —*Night Owl Romance Reviews*

"Opal Carew brings erotic romance to a whole new level. . . . She writes a compelling romance and sets your senses on fire with her love scenes!" —*Reader to Reader*

Secret Ties

Secret Ties

Opal Carew

St. Martin's Griffin

New York

SECRET TIES. Copyright © 2009 by Elizabeth Batten-Carew. All rights reserved. Printed in the United States of America. For information, address St. Martin's Press, 175 Fifth Avenue, New York, N.Y. 10010.

www.stmartins.com

Library of Congress Cataloging-in-Publication Data

Carew, Opal.
    Secret ties / Opal Carew.—1st ed.
        p.   cm.
    ISBN-13: 978-0-312-38480-7
    ISBN-10: 0-312-38480-7
    1. Sexual dominance and submission—Fiction.   I. Title.
    PR9199.4.C367S43   2009
    813'.6—dc22

                                        2009007372

First Edition: July 2009

10   9   8   7   6   5   4   3   2   1

This book is dedicated to

Colette,

*a warm, intelligent, and
very special woman
whom I admire very much,*

and to

Pat, Tyler, and Josh,

*the three special
men in her life.*

Acknowledgments

I would like to thank a very helpful friend, Ann, for giving me some wonderful insights into the world of BDSM and how loving a relationship can be between those in the lifestyle. My talks with Ann helped me come up with some very interesting ideas for the book, and also helped bring Max to life in my head (and, hopefully, in these pages).

Thank you to my great critiquers, Colette and Mark, my amazing editor, Rose, and my wonderful agent, Emily.

Mark, Matt, and Jason, you are the best, and I love you always.

One

Summer stared at the row of penises laid out in front of her—seven inches tall, standing straight up, and made of chocolate. Some dark chocolate, some milk chocolate, a couple of white chocolate, and a few where she'd experimented and created a pale flesh tone made from a combination of white and milk chocolate with a dab of red.

There was a constant thrum of voices in the large convention hall. Several people streamed by the table, some glancing at the erotic chocolates she had neatly arranged on the table, but most heading straight to the stack of books to Summer's right. Tanya's books. Summer glanced at Tanya, her friend the erotic romance author. Tanya smiled and closed the book she'd just finished signing, then handed it to the eager couple standing in front of her.

"I loved your last book," the young woman said. "I hope this one is just as sexy."

Tanya grinned, with a glint in her eye. "If anything, it's even sexier. I don't think you'll be disappointed."

Tanya wasn't kidding. Summer had read it, red-cheeked through the whole thing, but totally engrossed. She'd never read a book about submission and bondage before, and she'd had no idea her friend knew so much about it, but then Tanya had always been full of surprises.

She glanced at the scintillating cover of Tanya's latest book, showing a leather-clad man with tight abs and a muscular chest. The hero of the book—well, the main one—was very well-endowed. Summer had had more than a few intensely sexy dreams with him as the star since reading this particular book.

She glanced at Tanya, signing another book. She wondered about the type of life Tanya lived now. Did she go off with multiple men and actually experience the threesomes and moresomes she detailed in her stories? Summer couldn't imagine doing that, but she admired Tanya for having the guts to do it or even just to write about it. Summer had read in the acknowledgments that a particular man, whom she referred to simply as M, had helped her with her research. Just how in-depth had that research been?

Tanya closed the book and handed it to the woman in front of her. The woman smiled broadly and clutched the book to her chest, then grasped her husband's hand and led him away, further into the "den of iniquity," as Shane had teasingly called it when he heard Summer was going to Chicago, two hours from her home in Port Smith, to attend this trade show dedicated to adult entertainment.

She glanced around the dimly lit convention hall at the neat rows of booths lining the aisleways—booths with brightly colored, penis-shaped vibrators, glass dildos, skimpy lingerie, leather boots, feathers, ropes . . . and, of course, the booth she and Tanya shared, bursting with erotic chocolate and stacks of erotic romance books. But it sure was a long way from her little chocolate shop in an upscale hotel in a small town.

Summer adjusted the chocolate suckers in front of her—cocksuckers, which were small chocolate penises on a stick—into neat rows, then shifted her attention to the stacks of Tanya's books and straightened them into neat piles.

The people gathered around her booth were no longer looking at the goods on the tables. They were watching the stage and the two women on it. One was the flamboyant mistress of ceremonies, who wore a slinky, low-cut red velvet dress with a feather boa coiled around her neck and introduced herself as Mistress Cassie. The other woman wore . . . well, nothing, really. She did have a G-string . . . maybe . . . but mostly a few leather straps and links of metal draped around her rib cage from a harness over her shoulders. They did nothing to hide her small but pert breasts—which was odd because the show guidelines had stated no nudity. She also wore a bridle on her head with a bright-colored feather on top.

The MC had a small riding crop, and she commanded the feathered woman to prance around the stage with light slaps across her behind. Summer dragged her gaze from the stage and glanced around at the people watching with interest.

She felt a prickle down the back of her neck and glanced up to see a tall, devastatingly handsome man staring at her. He had dark eyes and black hair, cropped short and spiky. His square jaw, shadowed lightly, framed full lips, and a diamond glittered in one earlobe, making her think of a pirate prince.

Her gaze jerked away, then rested on the chocolates in

front of her, only to realize she was staring at a life-size chocolate erection. She glanced back at the man to find him grinning at her, as if to say, *It doesn't measure up to mine.* The very thought made her flush.

He smiled at her again, his eyes twinkling. She just gaped at him, totally blown away by his astounding, raw male magnetism. He wore a black leather jacket in a blazer style, which was rugged yet at the same time elegant. His dark eyes held her mesmerized, until the focus of those eyes strayed down her body, lingering on her breasts—setting a fire within her that threatened to blaze out of control. The rest of her was hidden from sight by the table, but her nipples hardened at his frank male interest, and she felt her insides melt, liquid heat gathering between her legs. She allowed her gaze to stray past his muscular shoulders to his broad chest and down to his narrow waist, then flicker over the front of his pants, wondering at the size of the male member he was hiding in those black jeans.

Good heavens, that wasn't like her. She glanced back to his face. To her horror, he smiled knowingly, and her cheeks flushed in embarrassment.

He stepped toward the table, and her breath caught. Was he going to talk to her? Maybe proposition her as several men had Tanya already? What would she possibly say to him?

Tanya glanced his way, and her lips turned up in a huge smile.

"Max."

The gorgeous hunk took Tanya's hand and kissed it. A pang of jealousy lanced through Summer. Which was *insane.*

"I see your book is doing well," he said.

The women in the line waiting to meet Tanya watched Max with wide eyes. He could have passed for a cover model.

Tanya winked. "Thanks to you."

Max? Was he M from the acknowledgments?

Her gaze shifted to his crotch, which had seemed to have become an obsession with her, and after a lingering perusal shifted away again and locked on to his dark eyes, glittering with amusement.

"So who's your friend?" Max asked.

Tanya held out her hand to Summer and drew her forward.

"Max Delaney, I'd like you to meet my very best friend, Summer Anderson. We've known each other since kindergarten. Unfortunately, since I've moved away from Port Smith, I hardly ever see her anymore." She smiled warmly at Summer. "Listen, honey, keep Max company while I finish signing books for these nice people, will you?"

There were about five people waiting in line.

"Sure." Summer smiled at Max as she moved to the edge of the table to give Tanya more room in the small space. Max moved with her. She glanced at him, unsure what to say. It was hard enough to hear over the constant din in the huge convention hall.

"You're just in Chicago for the weekend?"

She nodded. "Tanya invited me for the show."

"You make chocolates?"

She nodded again, feeling a bit like a bobble-head doll.

He picked up one of the full-size penises and gazed at it. Her cheeks heated.

"I don't usually make . . . uh . . . this kind of thing."

"They look very good. I especially like the flesh-toned ones. They look very real."

It was an odd sight, him standing there holding a penis in his hand.

"Would you like one?" Oh, man, what was she thinking? Why would he want one? "Uh . . . to give to your girl-friend." Oh, great. Now it sounded like she was trying to find out if he was available.

He pulled his wallet from his back pocket.

"Oh, no. I didn't mean . . . ," she stuttered.

He pulled out three tens and laid them on the table.

"You're a friend of Tanya's, so . . . please just consider it a gift," Summer said.

Oh, God, first she got caught staring at his crotch and now she was giving him chocolate penises. He must think her a complete nut job.

"How can I refuse small-town hospitality?" He smiled and put away his money.

"So, you two seem to be getting along." Tanya glanced at the penis in Max's hand. "Aren't they gorgeous? I told her she should charge more than fifteen dollars."

Tanya had suggested twenty-five or thirty, but Summer had been afraid people wouldn't pay that much, and she didn't want to take them home again. They weren't the kind of thing she'd sell in her store. This certainly wasn't the kind of thing she normally did, but when Tanya invited her along to the convention, Summer figured, What the heck? She might as well have fun with it.

"She wouldn't let me pay her at all." Max turned to Sum-mer. "The least you can do is let me buy you both a drink after the show."

Summer hesitated. She glanced at Tanya.

"Of course we'll join you for drinks," Tanya said. "It might be pretty late, though."

He shrugged, then took Tanya's hand and kissed it. "I don't mind waiting for two beautiful ladies."

Tanya laughed, and Summer noticed a slight flush on her cheeks. *She's just as affected by him as I am.* The realization sliced through her. Maybe her friend wanted to have some alone time with Max. Disappointment trickled through her. She'd have one drink with them, then excuse herself. She didn't intend to be a third wheel.

Tanya glanced at her watch. "Oh, I've got to go. My talk is in five minutes."

"Good luck," Summer said.

Tanya rested her hand on Max's forearm. "You coming to give me moral support?"

"Absolutely." Max followed her, and they disappeared into the crowd.

"Do you make these?"

Summer glanced up from giving change to the woman who'd just bought three cocksuckers and one of Tanya's books to see Mistress Cassie, the MC from the stage show, in her long—and very low-cut—red velvet dress, holding one of the cellophane-wrapped dark chocolate penises in her satin-gloved hand. It was difficult not to stare at the huge portion of her large, round breasts revealed by the neckline that plunged to her waist.

"I . . . uh . . . yes," she said, keeping her gaze firmly on Mistress Cassie's face, not the overflow of breasts spilling from her dress. Summer felt dwarfed beside this woman.

"They're very good. Great details."

Summer glanced around, a little embarrassed at how the woman was scrutinizing the penis.

"And these . . ." Mistress Cassie picked up one of the flesh-toned ones. "The color is awesome. It looks so real."

"Thank you."

Mistress Cassie opened her small, beaded bag and drew out a twenty-dollar bill, then handed it to Summer.

"And they're a steal at that price. Oh, I'll take a couple of these, too." She picked up two milk chocolate cocksuckers and handed Summer another five to make up the difference. "Listen, I've decided to interview a few of the vendors onstage . . . you know, to let people know what's available at the show. I'd like to do you." She smiled. "We could do it right now."

"Oh, I don't think so. Maybe you want to interview Tanya. She's an author, and it's her booth."

"Nonsense."

Summer turned around to see Tanya stepping behind the table.

"You go. I'll watch the booth." Tanya nudged Summer forward.

"I'm not really comfortable—"

"Don't worry, honey," Mistress Cassie said. "I'll do most of the talking, and people will be dying for your chocolate once I'm done."

She took Summer's hand, and Summer felt herself propelled through the convention hall, then up onto the stage. Mistress Cassie waved over a stagehand, dressed in black jeans and T-shirt, and handed him the full-size chocolate penis, then murmured some instructions and rejoined Summer.

"Go ahead and sit down." Mistress Cassie pointed to a set of three tall stools in the middle of the stage as she picked up a microphone.

"Hello, everyone," she said into the mike. "I'm Mistress Cassie, and I'm your mistress of ceremonies for the show." She gestured to the opposite side of the stage, and Summer noticed pony-girl, now dressed in a skimpy black leather-and-chain outfit—but with all the main bits covered—approaching center stage. "And this is Vex."

Vex bowed, then sat on the free stool to their right. Summer wondered what she'd gotten herself into. The chocolate penises had been just for fun. She'd never intended to end up onstage in some crazy sex show.

"Vex, do you know who I have here?" Mistress Cassie indicated Summer. She felt her cheeks flush as faces in the crowd turned to her.

"No, Mistress. Who is this lovely woman?"

"Her name is Summer Anderson, and she sells chocolates at the show. And not just ordinary chocolates." She held out one of the suckers to Vex, and the other woman took it.

Vex smiled devilishly. "They look . . . delicious."

"Summer, what do you call these?"

"Uh . . ." She felt her pulse pounding past her temples. "Those are . . . cocksuckers."

Mistress Cassie smiled. "Really?"

She plucked the ribbon from around the stick and peeled away the cellophane, then wrapped her lips around the sucker. Vex did the same. Both women made a big show of pulsing up and down on the suckers, and the crowd watched avidly.

Vex drew the sucker from her mouth and flicked her tongue over the tip. "Mmm. It is delicious."

"Summer also has these wonderful—"

"Mistress?"

"What is it, Vex?"

Vex pointed toward the curtain behind them. "Look."

Mistress Cassie and Summer both turned toward the curtain. Sticking out from between the fabric panels was a naked penis. Summer's eyes widened, then she realized it wasn't a real one. It was one of hers. But the audience couldn't tell that. Several made surprised sounds. Many laughed and twittered.

"Vex, go check it out," Mistress Cassie instructed.

Vex stood up and approached the curtain and stared at the penis. She leaned over to get a close look, giving the audience a great view of her mostly naked behind, then she crouched down beside the penis. She leaned forward and gave it a lick. Several men in the audience groaned.

"Mmm. I like it." She flicked her tongue over the tip several times, then swirled her tongue around the head. "It's very nice."

"Let me try." Mistress Cassie approached the curtain and crouched down on the other side, facing Vex, then she licked the shaft. "You're right."

The two women licked up and down the shaft, and their tongues toyed with the tip, occasionally meeting in the process. Mistress Cassie wrapped her hand around the base of the shaft, and Vex moved aside as Mistress Cassie swallowed the cock into her mouth. She went deep, then drew back, then bobbed up and down several times.

"Now, that is what I call a cocksucker."

She plucked the cock from whoever, or whatever, was holding it in place behind the curtain. The audience chuckled.

"Aren't we the cocksuckers?" Vex asked.

"I suppose you're right." Mistress Cassie winked at the audience as she held up the slightly melted penis on the palm of her hand. "If you want a sweet and very sexy treat, you'll find these chocolate penises at the booth Summer shares with Tanya Doyle, the erotica author. Their booth is four to the left of the west entrance."

Vex stepped up to Summer and gestured for her to stand up.

"Summer," Mistress Cassie said, "thank you for joining us."

Summer nodded. True to her word, Mistress Cassie had done almost all the talking. Vex led Summer off the stage as Mistress Cassie began announcing the other events for the evening.

Summer walked down the steps from the stage and headed toward the edge of the convention hall, trying to avoid the people who had been gaping at the spectacle onstage. That was hands down the oddest thing she'd ever participated in. She dodged around the end booth and relaxed a little when she saw there weren't many people along this aisle.

"Hey, pretty lady," said a slurry male voice. "I saw you up onstage."

Two

Summer glanced up to see a muscular man of average height, holding a plastic cup full of beer. He had tousled blond hair and wore jeans and a striped blue shirt.

She nodded and tried to step past him, but he side-stepped.

"You know, you're a really good cocksucker."

"Oh, no, that wasn't me. That was—"

"I mean, like . . . really good." He flung his arm around her shoulder, and she felt a sense of panic. He leaned in toward her as if to tell her a secret, and she could smell the beer on his breath. "I was thinking, maybe you and me . . . we could go somewhere, and you know . . ." He took another sip of his beer, spilling a little on her shirt. "That thing on the stage was chocolate, but . . . ." He snickered. "I've got the real thing. Whaddya say?"

She took a calming breath and said, "No, thank you."

She stared at him, eyes wide, wondering if she pushed his arm away whether he'd let her go or get belligerent.

"Ah now, pretty lady." He stumbled a little, then leaned on her shoulder. "You really are a pretty lady. Did I tell you that?"

She nodded, wishing he'd just let her go.

"I didn't mean to scare you. It's just that you really seem to like sucking cock, and . . . you obviously like sex . . ." He waved his arm around, encompassing their surroundings. "I can tell . . . you being here and all." He grinned at her. "So, c'mon. Let's go."

"Summer? There you are."

She glanced up to see Max Delaney standing just a few feet away. Summer had never been so glad to see anyone in her life.

The guy fawning over her stared at Max, who was taller than him by a head. The man immediately withdrew his arm from her shoulder, and she stepped toward Max. The guy held his flattened palms forward.

"Hey, man. Sorry. Didn't know she was here with someone." He glanced at her. "You *are* here with him, right?"

"Of course," she said, then raised her lips to give Max a light kiss on the cheek to be more convincing.

Max caught her under the chin and lifted, then captured her mouth. The feel of his lips pressed against hers, coaxing her mouth to respond, was overwhelming. His tongue pressed between her lips, and she opened for him, welcoming him inside. His tongue tangled with hers, guiding it into a seductive dance. His hand slipped behind her head, and he held her gently as he mastered her mouth. Finally, he drew away and she stared into his simmering charcoal eyes, dazed.

"So you think maybe that woman in the skimpy little thingy is free?" asked the swaying blond man, his finger making X shapes, indicating the straps of Vex's costume.

"Vex is here with her husband," Max answered. "A big, burly guy."

"Damn. Okay, thanks, buddy." At that, he wandered around the corner, probably back to the bar.

"You know Vex?" Summer asked.

"Not really, but he doesn't know that."

Reluctantly, she stepped from the comfort of his arm around her. "Thank you, I . . . really appreciate you stepping in."

He smiled. "No problem. Would you like to get a drink, then look around the place?"

Thoughts of staring at big glass dildos with this man at her side sent her head into a spin. "I . . . uh . . . really shouldn't leave Tanya alone at the booth."

"Tanya was the one who suggested it. She thought you might want a break after your experience onstage."

Her cheeks heated anew. She really didn't want to face standing behind the booth with all those chocolate penises after watching Mistress Cassie and her friend working away at the one onstage.

"Okay, sure."

He offered his elbow, and she hooked her hand through it. He led her to the bar, and as she accepted the glass of orange juice and vodka, she realized a stiff drink was exactly what she needed, especially right before perusing sex toys with a tall, handsome stranger.

There were certainly all kinds of sex toys at this show. At one booth, a dark-haired woman in a black lace bustier and black leather pants chatted with a redhead sitting in a large swing. The dark-haired woman, whom Summer realized was manning the booth, helped the redhead attach straps around her thighs.

"This is totally adjustable," the dark-haired woman said.

"What do you think?" the redhead asked a burly blond man who stood watching. "Do you think it'll fit in the bedroom?"

"I'm sure we can make it fit." He practically drooled as she widened her legs and the dark-haired woman spun her around.

"You can see that this gives you a great deal of flexibility in positions." She gestured the man forward and encouraged him closer to his partner. "If you want it a little higher . . ." At her urging, he stepped between the redhead's thighs until his denim-clad crotch pressed against hers. "Actually, this is perfect for you."

The redhead wrapped her legs around him and leaned back. "Oh, this would be so fun."

Summer couldn't believe how open the redhead was. In a way, Summer admired her, but at the same time, she found it embarrassing to watch.

Max pressed his hand to her back. "Do you want to try the swing?"

"No, thank you." Actually, she would. She was definitely curious, but there was no way she would try it in public. It's not like she was one of these weird sex people. She was here just to have fun with her friend.

They passed an extensive display of lingerie, then she stopped at the next booth as her gaze fell on a stunning pair of black shoes with a sexy strap around the ankle. The heels looked to be about five inches tall and were made of shiny silver metal.

"Why don't you try them on?" Max asked.

She glanced at the price tag and balked. Four hundred dollars.

"I can't afford them."

"You don't have to buy them to try them on."

She had to admit, it would be fun to see what it was like to wear them. A clerk asked her size and showed up with a box a moment later. She took one from the tissue inside the box and handed it to Summer.

"Here, let me help." Max pulled a stool forward and held the shoe to Summer's foot. She pushed her toe in, and Max fastened the strap around her ankle. The feel of his fingers on her skin sent tingles through her. He lifted her other foot in his warm, masculine hand. He put the other shoe on her and fastened it. She almost sighed when he released her ankle to set her foot on the ground. He stood up and offered his hand, then drew her to her feet.

"They look stunning," he said.

She glanced in the mirror on the wall. They made her legs look long and . . . well, sexy. She walked toward the mirror, then turned around and walked away. As she glanced over her shoulder, she realized it made her butt look higher and round, but firm.

Oh man, she loved these shoes.

"They're very nice." She walked back and forth a few times, then sat back down and began unfastening them. She had to get them off before she decided she had to have them and blew four hundred bucks she couldn't afford.

They stopped in another booth that had erotic artwork, which was all quite beautiful. She admired the lengths of rhinestones in many brilliant colors at another booth.

"They're to replace your bra straps," said the woman behind the table. "See?" She peeled back her black camisole top enough to show where the rhinestone straps over her shoulders attached to her black bra.

"Very pretty."

As she and Max moved on to the next booth, Summer glanced at her watch. She'd left Tanya alone for almost an hour now, and she felt guilty.

"I should get back to the booth."

Max accompanied her, and when she arrived, she noticed all her chocolates were gone. Had Tanya started packing up for the evening?

"Did you have fun?" Tanya asked.

"Uh-huh." Summer glanced under the table as she stepped into the booth, but the boxes she'd brought the chocolates in were empty.

"Great news. Your stuff sold out. A huge crowd showed up after that bit on the stage . . . and the penises sold for about thirty dollars each."

"But how?"

"Well, more people wanted them than we could supply, so I . . . sort of let people bid on them."

"Tanya!"

She shrugged. "Well, why not?" She glanced at her watch. "You know, I'm about ready to call it a night, and you don't have any reason to stay here, so what do you say, Max? How about that drink?"

Although Max had politely invited both of them earlier, Summer assumed Tanya would rather have him to herself.

"I'll just head back to the room," Summer said. "I'll see you later."

"Summer, I thought you were going to join us," Tanya said.

"Well, I don't want to intrude." Especially since she had no idea what the relationship was between Tanya and Max.

"Nonsense." Tanya hooked her arm around Summer's. "You're coming with us."

Summer followed Tanya toward the elevators, intensely aware of Max behind her. They stepped inside and the doors closed. As she stood beside Max's tall, overwhelmingly masculine physique, it felt as though all the air had been sucked from the small space. She almost breathed a sigh of relief when the doors opened and they followed Max down the carpeted hallway. He stopped at the last door on the left and slipped his key card into the slot.

Summer followed Tanya into a large living room complete with a fireplace on one wall. The simple décor gave an air of elegance. Cream furniture with clean lines and a dove gray carpet were set off by vibrant artwork. Several green plants set around the space along with a bright-colored flower arrangement on the glass coffee table made the place feel homey. She gazed at the spectacular view of the glittering city lights beyond the large window.

"It's a lovely room," Summer said.

She settled into a cozy armchair, avoiding the couch and the possibility of winding up sitting next to Max. Tanya sat on the couch. At the sound of grating ice, Summer glanced around to see Max pulling a tall black bottle from an ice bucket. Expertly, he popped the cork, then poured bubbly liquid into three tall flute glasses sitting on the table beside the bucket. He handed a glass to Tanya, one to Summer, then raised his own.

"To your new book, Tanya. May it be wildly successful."

Tanya grinned widely and clinked her glass against his, then against Summer's. As Summer's glass brushed Max's with a light clink, she felt a tingle skitter down her arm, as though they had actually touched.

She sipped the champagne, enjoying the bubbles as they danced inside her mouth then down her throat.

"So what do you do when you're not at the Sex-à-la-Gala show, Summer?" Max asked.

Extremely conscious of his dark gaze on her face, she cleared her throat. "I own a chocolate shop. In a small hotel in Port Smith."

"Chocolate and sex. A natural combination." He smiled. "Thank you again for your gift."

Her cheeks flushed at the reminder. An image of Mistress Cassie and Vex licking and sucking on the chocolate penis shuddered through her mind. Somehow, she just couldn't imagine Max . . .

She toyed with the slender stem of her glass. "I don't usually . . . uh . . . I mean, usually I make truffles and chocolate roses . . . things like that, but Tanya wanted me to come to the show and suggested I make . . . uh . . ."

"Erotic chocolate," Tanya jumped in. "You should have heard her laugh when I suggested the chocolate penises. I'm surprised she actually did it. Too bad she didn't run with my idea of having chocolate vaginas, too."

Summer felt her face flush again.

Max smiled, and Summer's gaze lingered on his full lips and straight white teeth. That mouth looked so masculine . . . so strong. A quiver raced down her spine as she remembered what it felt like to be kissed by him. To feel those lips against hers, his tongue delving into her mouth with controlled confidence.

"People seemed to like what you had to offer."

He filled her glass again, and she realized she'd drained it. She took a sip of the bubbly liquid and felt it warm her throat. She wasn't used to champagne, and she could feel it relaxing her.

"You helped Tanya with her research on this book." Summer watched those full, masculine lips turn up in a smile again. She really liked his smile. "So you must know a lot about bondage."

"Not just bondage, honey," Tanya said. "BDSM."

Summer pursed her lips. "I don't really know a lot about . . . BDSM. People talk about whips and pain. The S and M stands for sado-masochism, doesn't it?" She couldn't imagine Tanya writing about people hurting other people.

"BDSM actually stands for a number of subdivisions of what used to be known as sado-masochism," Max explained. "This includes bondage, bondage and discipline, and Dominance and submission."

"Max is a very talented Dominant." Tanya winked at Summer. "That's Dominant with a capital D."

Max chuckled. "Dominant is always spelled with a capital D by those in the lifestyle."

"And submissive with a small s. I know." Tanya stroked his hand. "So I'll say you're Talented with a capital T."

He tipped his head in acknowledgment of the compliment.

Summer gazed at him, wondering if Tanya had played the game of submission and Dominance with Max.

The thought of Max, commanding and masculine, playing the role of the Dominant sent a quiver down her spine. What would it be like to be dominated by him? The very thought sent her pulse racing.

Her vivid imagination conjured an image of her standing before him naked, him fully clothed, and her kneeling in front of him and unzipping his pants, then reaching inside to draw out a long, hard cock, then wrapping her lips around it—

"Are we making you uncomfortable, Summer?" Tanya asked.

Summer's gaze jerked to her friend's face. "Uh . . . no, I just . . . don't really get it."

As much as the discussion triggered thoughts of hot, illicit sex with Max, she was sure that was more because of his strong masculine aura.

"Why would any woman want to be submissive to a man when we've fought so long to be recognized as strong and independent?"

"Summer, come here."

At Max's tone, Summer's gaze flew to his face. His dark eyes cut through her uncertainty as he spoke again. "Stand up and come over here."

His commanding tone was irresistible. She stood up and stepped toward him before she realized what she was doing.

She stopped in front of him, feeling a bit foolish, yet a part of her wanted to obey him. He seemed so utterly masculine, and that thrilled her.

"Fill my glass with champagne."

She drew in a deep breath, realizing she'd been worried—yet excited at the prospect—that he would order her to do something . . . illicit . . . even if just a kiss.

She turned toward the table, picked up the cold black bottle, and filled Max's glass.

"Now Tanya's," Max commanded.

She filled it, then stood there holding the bottle.

"Now put the bottle down and return to your seat."

She replaced the bottle on the table. Why had she waited for him to tell her to do that? She'd stood there holding it like a mindless idiot. It was as if she'd gone into a mode where she just waited for his commands, with no mind of her own.

She returned to her seat.

"You were just a submissive," Max said.

She nodded, not risking saying anything, afraid her voice would quaver.

"The Dominant-submissive relationship is all about the exchange of power. The submissive chooses to be controlled by the Dominant. The Dominant does not take away the rights of the submissive, she gives them freely.

"A submissive never has to do anything she doesn't want to do. You could have chosen at any time not to follow my commands."

Summer shrugged. "But they were innocuous. It didn't matter."

"Excuse me," Tanya interjected. "As fascinating as all this is, I need to use the little girls' room."

As soon as Tanya had disappeared down the hall, Max said, "And if I had ordered you to kneel down and perform oral sex on me, you wouldn't have done it."

"That's right." Of course she wouldn't have. Tanya had been sitting there and . . .

Shock permeated her body. Was it only because Tanya

had been a witness that she wouldn't have? If she had been alone with Max . . . if he had ordered her to . . .

Waves of need washed through her. Could it be that she *wanted* him to order her to do something unseemly? Something she wouldn't ordinarily consider?

She sucked in a deep breath. If Tanya had not been sitting there, how far would she have gone?

As Max watched her, interest flickered in his eyes.

"Summer. Come here."

Immediately, she obeyed him.

"Now, crouch down in front of me."

Her heart thumped loudly in her chest. Oh, God, he'd looked into her eyes and seen everything she'd been thinking.

Was he going to tell her to pull out his cock and suck it? She wouldn't do it. She couldn't.

She crouched down, their gazes locked.

The thought of his long, hard cock in her hand, pulsing with desire, overwhelmed her with need. She imagined the feel of it in her mouth, imagined running the tip of her tongue under the rim of his cock head.

They were eye to eye now. He leaned forward, bringing his face closer to her own until his mouth was a mere inch from hers. Her lips tingled with longing, wanting to be kissed by him. He stroked his hand along her neck, his touch powerful and overwhelming in its intensity.

Her pulse accelerated as they stayed like that several long, intense moments. Her nipples hardened, and liquid heat settled between her thighs. She wanted to feel his full, masculine lips on hers again. She wanted to scream at him to make her kiss him.

Why don't I just do it?

But she waited. Wanting him to command her. Wanting him to *control* her.

Finally, he closed the distance, capturing her mouth with his. His fingers stroked through her hair and curled around the back of her head as his tongue brushed her lips, then eased into her mouth in a gentle, coaxing caress. He explored her mouth with an assertive expertise that left her quivering.

"Well, I see I missed the fun stuff."

Max's fingers tightened around Summer's head, preventing her from jerking away at the sound of Tanya's voice. He continued the kiss, taking her breath away as his lips devoured hers with heady, erotic hunger.

When he released her, she gazed into his dark eyes, knowing he saw more than she wanted him to.

"Well, I have some things I need to get done before morning, so I'll just leave the two of you alone." Tanya grabbed her purse from the side table by the couch and walked toward the door.

"I'll come, too," Summer said, standing up.

"Summer, stay." Max smiled, his eyes warm and inviting.

It had been a request rather than a command, but she froze. Should she stay here alone with this stranger? If she did, she would start down a path she wasn't sure she wanted to follow, despite the curiosity and desire that stabbed through her.

Tanya grabbed Summer's arm and dragged her across the room.

"Give us a second, Max." Tanya smiled, then tugged Summer into the bedroom and closed the door.

"Honey, you two obviously have strong chemistry," Tanya said. "You should stay."

"But I don't even know him."

"It's not like he's a total stranger. He's a great guy—you can trust me on that. You'll have a fabulous time."

Summer's heart pounded in her chest as she stared at Tanya, torn between common sense and a strange yearning to do something totally out of character . . . like staying to see just where things might lead with Max Delaney.

"You're curious about this Dominant-submissive thing, I can tell . . . and believe me, Max will be the best one to show you the ropes, so to speak. What better way to explore something new and exciting than a weekend fling? Monday you go back to Port Smith and your usual life with no one the wiser. You can stash this away as an exciting memory."

Summer stared at the big bed and quivered at the thought of Max overwhelming her senses with his intense masculinity. She could imagine his lips caressing her body, his hard body possessing hers as she surrendered to him.

A weekend fling. No one at home will ever know.

It had been a long time since she'd had any kind of sex, let alone kinky, exciting sex that involved her submitting to the whims of another. Especially someone as potently sexy as Max Delaney.

Domination.

Her heart pounded. She wondered if Max had handcuffs somewhere around here. The thought of cold steel cuffs gripping her wrists, holding her down, sent her pulse skyrocketing.

"So what do you say?" Tanya asked.

Summer took a deep breath, then nodded.

Three

"Summer, do you have a man back home?" Max sat on the couch across from her.

She stared at her lap as she dragged her finger along her knee. "Actually, there are two. . . ."

He smiled as his eyebrow arched upward. "Really?"

"No . . . I mean, I'm not involved with both of them . . . neither of them, actually . . . I just . . ."

"Would like to be?"

She glanced at him and nodded.

He picked up his glass and swirled it around. "Then why aren't you?"

"It's complicated. They're best friends, and . . . I'm friends with both of them. If I go out with one . . ." She shrugged.

"You're afraid you'll break up their friendship?" He took a sip of his drink.

She nodded. "And I wouldn't know how to choose between them anyway."

"Why not go out with both?"

"Both?"

He leaned forward. "So we're clear, I mean have a three-some. Then you don't have to choose."

Her cheeks flushed. "Oh, no. I couldn't do that."

He smiled. "Really? I think there are a great many things you might do that you don't think you could . . . in the right circumstances."

His dark gaze bored into her until she found herself squirming in her seat. He placed his drink on the glass table.

"Summer, come sit over here."

He didn't say it in his authoritative voice, but she obeyed anyway, standing up and moving to the couch, then sitting beside him.

She gazed at him and felt overwhelmed by the intense scrutiny of his dark eyes. She felt as though, at this moment, she were the entire focus of his world. As if he could see everything about her . . . knew everything there was to know about her. Even things she didn't know about herself.

He stroked his finger along her cheek, and exciting tingles danced through her body like fireflies on a summer's night. His fingers glided through her long auburn hair, and he drew her forward. When his mouth met hers in a soft brush of lips, then moved with a delicate pressure, she drew in a breath and melted against him.

His tongue moved inside her mouth in long, sexy strokes . . . exploring . . . caressing. He wrapped his arms around her and drew her close to his hard, rigid body. Her nipples blossomed into tight nubs, pressing into his muscular chest.

His lips brushed against her ear. "You are a sexy, beautiful woman, Summer. I want to make love to you. To release the passion within you."

She gazed at him, a prisoner to his sinfully sexy charcoal eyes. Her lips longed for his again.

"I know you don't really know me," he said, "but if you'll give in to your desires and trust me, I'll take you on a journey you'll never forget." He pressed his fingertip to her lips, then traced the lower curve. "Just remember, you decide."

"I decide?"

His lips captured hers again, and she melted against him. Her arms encircled his neck, and she clung to him. He was so strong. So masculine. So sexy!

"Are you ready?"

Was she? A part of her wanted to race to the door and run back to the security of her room. To flee the sudden urges turning her into a raging mass of desire.

She nodded, then cleared her throat. "Yes. I'm ready."

His smile broadened. "Good."

Then his smile faded and his gaze sharpened.

"Stand up."

She pushed herself to her feet and stood before him.

"Turn around."

Slowly, she turned around, continuing until she faced him again, aware of his gaze gliding over her body, searing her with his frank male scrutiny.

"Unbutton your blouse."

Oh, God, can I really do this?

But her fingers, with a mind of their own, flicked open the top button, then the next. As her blouse parted to reveal the swell of her breasts beneath, she sucked in a breath. She felt the heat of a flush start down her neck and across her chest. Still her fingers moved downward until all the buttons were undone and the blouse fell open, revealing her breasts encased in black lace.

"Take off the blouse and fold it neatly, then put it on the chair."

She slid the garment off her shoulders, then folded it, the ordinary act keeping her mind off the fact that she had just stripped off her top at a stranger's command. An intensely sexy stranger.

"Now unbutton your skirt and drop it to the floor."

She reached behind her and unfastened the button and dragged down the zipper, then glided the waistband past her hips and let the skirt fall to the floor.

Tanya had talked her into wearing a garter belt and black stockings, in keeping with the theme of the show. Seeing the simmering heat in Max's eyes as he stared at the naked white skin at the tops of her thighs, she was glad she had.

"Now step out of the skirt."

Summer took a step forward, out of the ring of fabric.

"Turn around and pick up the skirt."

She turned around, then leaned over, intensely aware that the pose gave Max a sexy view of her derrière, almost totally bare in the black lace thong she wore. Her fingers grasped the black fabric of her skirt, but she waited a few seconds before she stood up, surprised at her own wantonness.

She rose, holding the skirt in her hand, awaiting his next order.

"Fold it, and put it on top of your blouse, then come over here."

Once she'd disposed of the skirt, she walked toward

him. Would he ask her to take off her bra now? Then her panties?

He poured some champagne into the two flute glasses in front of him and held one out to her. She took the glass and raised it to her lips, took a sip, then another. The bubbly liquid filled her mouth and tickled her throat. She was still feeling the effects from the two glasses she'd had earlier, but she knew that had nothing to do with her actions. When she finished the glass, she glanced at the table, wanting to put down the flute. He nodded and she placed it on the table.

"Summer, you can decide the small things, or leave them to me. It's up to you. What's important is following my direct orders."

She nodded, wondering what his next direct order would be.

"Go to the chair behind you and sit down."

Once she was sitting comfortably, he said, "Now stroke your breasts."

A quiver ran through her as she leaned back in the chair and stroked her fingers over her breasts. They felt warm and round. It felt so strange doing this in front of someone.

Max's gaze seared her.

"Take off the bra."

She flicked the strap at the back, and the hooks unlatched. She dropped the straps from her shoulders, then drew in a deep breath, feeling sinfully naughty as she slid the lace garment forward. Cool air brushed her sensitive skin as she freed her naked breasts to his hot and hungry view. Her nipples strained forward, hard and needy.

"Now touch the nipples. Show me what you like."

She stroked a fingertip over one, then dabbed at it. Molten heat jolted through her . . . straight to her vagina. She stroked the other breast, then glided over the hard nipple. His heated gaze followed every movement of her fingers, driving her excitement to a sizzling level.

She licked her fingertips and stroked over one hard nub, then the other, wishing the dampness were from Max's tongue.

"Very nice. Take off your panties."

Summer stood up and tucked her thumbs under the elastic of her panties, but she hesitated. Could she really do this? Get totally naked in front of this man while he sat there fully clothed and watched her?

"Take them off," he said firmly.

Her fingers worked the panties down her legs to her ankles without waiting for her brain to catch up, then she kicked the flimsy garment away. Now she stood practically naked in front of him. In fact, she felt more exposed wearing just the black garter belt and stockings. Her cheeks began to burn as his gaze stroked over her auburn pubic curls, framed in lace and silk, then meandered over her breasts again.

"Good girl. You have an exceptionally beautiful body, Summer. I love looking at it."

She flushed again, this time in delight because she'd pleased him.

"Come kneel in front of me."

She stepped toward him, aware of his simmering gaze taking in every part of her, then knelt in front of him, wondering what he would do next. Wanting him to touch her hard, needy nipples. She had to stop herself from leaning forward.

"Touch my face, Summer."

She reached forward and stroked his cheek. The raspy heat of him excited her.

"Kiss me. Passionately. Show me how much you want me."

She slid her arms around his neck and matched her mouth to his. She licked his lips, then eased her tongue between them, into his mouth. Her lips moved on his as she explored his moist heat. His tongue coiled with hers, and her breath escaped as a primal need built within her. She tightened her arms around him, her mouth moving frantically on his. Her naked breasts pressed against his hard chest. The leather of his jacket rasped against her nipples. Her hand stroked down his chest, past his belt, to the bulge straining in his pants. She stroked over it, amazed at the length of the hardness.

His hand grasped hers.

"You are a naughty girl. I didn't give you permission to do that."

Her gaze locked with his.

"Now, I will have to punish you."

She sucked in a breath. Punishment? She drew back a little, and the anxiety must have shown in her eyes because he drew her forward for a kiss.

"It's all right, sweetheart. Remember, this is play. The punishment I'm talking about isn't whips or chains . . . though if you want that, let me know." He grinned wickedly. "I think now is a good time to mention safe words. You will pick a word that will tell me you want me to stop immediately. It shouldn't be a word like 'no' or 'stop.' In our roles, you might want to struggle or pretend to want something to stop. The safe word allows us to explore interesting scenarios and play our roles to the fullest, while assuring you that you can stop things at any time. Understand?"

She nodded.

"So pick a word. Something easy to remember."

"I don't know . . . I . . . uh . . ."

"What's the first word that comes to mind?"

Her blank mind thrust a word forward.

"Cat."

"Okay." He smiled. "Cat it is. Now, I want you to use that word within the next few minutes, just to assure yourself it works."

She nodded.

"Okay. From now on, you will call me Master. Understood?"

Her eyes widened, but she nodded again.

"I want to hear you say it."

"Yes, Master."

"Good." He patted his lap. "Now about that punishment. Stretch over my knee."

She drew in air, which suddenly felt scarce, but she did as she was told. Her naked behind exposed to him . . . excited her. His hand stroked over the curve of her buttocks, from her thigh to her lower back, then down the other side. Her skin tingled, wanting to feel his hand stroke . . . wanting to feel it slap against her. Shock careened through her at the realization.

He lifted his hand and his palm connected with her hot skin with a light smacking sound. Her vagina clenched at the tingling sensation across her ass. His hand smacked against her skin again, and she held back a moan.

"Summer, remember the safe word?"

His hand connected with her backside again, and heat surged through her.

If she said the safe word, he would stop.

But she didn't want him to stop.

His hand came down a little harder this time, smarting more than tingling.

"Summer?"

Moisture pooled in her vagina, and she was afraid it would begin to drip down her thighs.

He smacked again.

"Cat," she murmured.

He stroked over her heated buttock. Soothing. His hands slid around her shoulders and he helped her up.

"Good girl."

He smiled as his finger stroked under her chin and tipped it up, then he kissed her. Gentle and affectionate.

"Now that I've punished you, shall we continue?"

She'd said the safe word, so this was his way of offering to continue their roles or stop entirely.

"Continue, Master."

He smiled. "Now that deserves a reward." He patted the seat beside him. "Sit down."

She sat down and he shifted to his knees. For the first time, he stroked her breast, then cupped it in his big, warm hand. She sighed, her eyelids drooping downward . . . then they popped open again as something hot and moist covered her other nipple.

His tongue teased her hard nub, then he sucked lightly. She moaned at the exquisite pleasure. He shifted to her other breast. His tongue twirled around her nipple, then he sucked it hard.

Her fingers raked through his hair as she pulled him tighter to her breast.

"What would you like right now?" he asked.

She stared at him, still wearing his black leather jacket, black striped shirt, and jeans. Her gaze ran down his chest, then rested on his ever growing bulge.

"I want to see you naked."

He smiled. "Then undress me."

He stood up, and so did she. She grasped the soft leather and eased his jacket off his shoulders, then pushed it down his arms until it dropped away. She reached for the top button of his shirt, then flicked it open. As she moved to the next, she licked her lips, anxious to see his hard, male chest. Her heart thumped while she revealed more hard flesh as she released button after button. She ran her hand over his hard pecs, then down his chiseled abs. She stopped at his belt, then tugged his shirt free and released the last button, then thrust the shirt over his shoulders . . . realizing at the last minute that his cuffs were still fastened. He chuckled and released them himself, then tugged his arms from the sleeves and tossed the shirt aside.

She unfastened his belt buckle, then tugged down his zipper. In a moment, she would see the large cock he hid within. The outline she glimpsed was very impressive. Once she unhooked the waistband, the pants fell to the floor with a thump. He stepped out of them and divested himself of his socks with two quick movements.

Now he stood before her in only his black briefs. She grasped the elastic of his waistband and pulled it forward. The biggest, longest cock she'd ever seen fell forward. It had a bulbous head and a long, thick shaft with prominent veins that seemed to pulse with life. She slid the briefs down past his ankles. He lifted one foot at a time to allow her to pull the cotton garment free.

She knelt in front of him and reached for his hard cock, longing to feel it.

"Summer, stop."

She stared up at him in amazement.

"You've had your reward. Now stand up."

She obeyed.

"You want to touch me?"

She nodded.

"You're forgetting already. How do you respond?"

"Yes, Master." Excitement tingled through her at the words.

"Do you want me to touch you?"

It became difficult to breathe.

"Yes, Master."

He smiled. "Sit down on the couch."

She did so immediately.

"Summer, are you wet?"

Her cheeks flamed with heat, but she nodded, then caught herself.

"Yes, Master."

"Show me."

Show me? The only way to do that would be . . .

Slowly, she spread her knees, exposing her naked labia. He stared at her, and her insides seemed to melt. His hand wrapped around his huge, rigid cock, and he stroked it. Jealousy surged through her. She wanted to stroke it. To suck it.

"I don't see wet," he said.

How could he not?

"Show me," he insisted.

She slid her fingers along her lower lips and drew them apart, exposing her wet opening.

Max could see the light glistening from her wet slit, and his cock nearly drove him crazy wanting to thrust into her.

"I don't see it." He wondered how she would respond.

She lowered her lids in a most enticing way.

"Maybe you should feel it, Master."

Oh, man, hearing her call him Master was a thrill. Hearing her ask him to touch her wet pussy made his pulse accelerate.

"You are getting very bold. I might have to gag you if you speak out of turn."

It was a playful warning. He wouldn't gag her . . . tonight. Tomorrow . . . maybe. Except then he wouldn't hear her call him Master. Of course, the thought of a ball gag—or better yet, a gag with a cock head filling her mouth—made his cock expand. Or a gag with a hole that held her mouth open so he could slide his cock into it . . . and fuck her delicious mouth. He had to hold back a groan.

"Slide your fingers into your pussy."

He watched as she dipped her index and middle fingers into her wet slit.

"Stroke inside." He had to hold himself rigid against his cock's urgent plea. "Deeper."

Her fingers thrust deeper into her hot pussy.

"Stroke over your clit."

She obeyed, and soon her fingertips glided over her little button in a rhythmic movement. Her breathing, heavy now, clearly showed her heightened arousal. She was getting close.

"Pull them out. Now."

She groaned at his command but obeyed.

He knelt in front of her and wrapped his hand around her wrist.

When Summer felt Max's mouth surround her wet fingers, she nearly lost it. She'd been so close to orgasm when he'd stopped her.

"Do not come unless I tell you to. Do you understand?"

No.

"Yes, Master."

Could she really stop herself from coming? Could she come on command?

He knelt on the floor in front of her and kissed first one breast, then the other. She clung to his head and murmured softly.

Would he punish her for being so bold?

Maybe. She remembered the sting of his hand on her ass. It had been . . . erotic. Not the pain—his playful slaps hadn't been hard enough to cause pain—but they had caused an exciting, stimulating tingle across her flesh.

She pulled his head tighter against her breast.

"Suck harder, Master."

At the sudden tug against her nipple, she gasped.

"Yes." She moaned as his tongue swirled over her sensitive, aroused aureole. "Oh, Master, I want to suck your cock. I want you to fuck me. Hard and fast." She couldn't believe the words coming from her mouth.

He lifted his head from her breast. "If I didn't know better, I'd think you want to be punished again."

His gaze fixed on her face, and he grinned.

Suddenly, his hands grasped her hips and she felt herself flipped up and over. She was ass up with his bare knees under her abdomen. A sharp smacking sound accompanied the heat of a smarting sting on her behind.

"Ohhhhh."

He smacked her again. Her whole body trembled with need. One more smack, then she felt herself rolled onto the couch with her legs spread wide. Max lifted her knees over his shoulders, and she felt moisture seep down her thighs. His finger stroked over her slit, and she arched against him.

He chuckled.

"I'm going to lick you. I'm going to make you come."

That certainly wouldn't be hard.

"But you won't come until I tell you."

Anxiety wound through her. Could she contain herself until his command?

The tip of his tongue dabbed against her swollen clit, and she moaned. His fingers dipped into her opening and stroked inside her. Heat swelled through her. He licked her clit, and she moaned again. Still his finger stroked her inner walls. Pressure built within her. . . . He sucked on her. A rising flood of pleasure. He swirled his tongue around and around.

She was so close. How could she hold back?

His fingers thrust deep inside her, just as she wanted his giant cock to do, and he sucked deeply on her clit.

"Oh, God. Oh, Master, please let me come."

"Mmm. Say it again."

"Oh, Master—"

He sucked harder.

"I want to . . ."

He stroked inside, and the pleasure became almost unbearable.

". . . come . . ."

He lifted his head and his gaze captured hers. Long moments passed as his fingers stroked her inner walls.

Her G-spot. Damn it, he knew where it was!

He stroked and stroked. Insufferable heat. Intense, painful pleasure seared every nerve end.

"Now, Summer. Come for me."

"Ohhhh . . . ," she wailed. "Master . . ."

Liquid flooded from inside her as her body shuddered in the most intense orgasm she'd ever experienced. Then she blacked out.

Max stared at her in shock. He stroked her cheek.

"Summer?"

Her eyelids fluttered open, and he sighed in relief.

"Are you all right?" he asked.

She smiled. "Yes, Master."

His cock twitched at her words.

"That was incredible." Her breathy words made him smile.

He'd heard of women passing out from the pleasure of orgasm but had never witnessed it personally. God, she was so responsive. So incredibly sexy.

He hadn't been sure she'd be able to hold off her orgasm until his command, but she had proven to be a perfect sub. Her desire to obey his commands was stronger than the demands of her own body.

"You did exceptionally well, Summer. Choose your reward."

She glanced at his swollen cock and licked her lips.

"I want to touch your cock, Master. I want to suck it."

He sat on the couch beside her. "Do it, Summer."

She slipped from the couch and knelt in front of him. The delicate touch of her fingers on his straining cock nearly sent him over the edge, but with as much discipline as she had shown, he held back. She wrapped her warm fingers around him and stroked his shaft, gliding the length of him, then she leaned forward and her warm mouth surrounded him.

"Your mouth feels good on me, Summer."

She swallowed him deep, and he groaned. Hot moisture surrounded his cock. It pulsed, begging for release. She glided back, then swallowed him again. His fingers entwined in her glossy auburn hair and cupped her head. She dove down and back, down and back, until he thought he would lose control.

"Now, Summer. I need to fuck you."

He pulled himself from her mouth and rolled her onto the floor. He prowled over her and pressed his cock head against her sopping wet pussy. Before he drove deep, he captured her gaze.

"I'm going to fuck you."

He waited, holding back the primal animal inside. Would she say the safe word?

"Yes, Master," she murmured. "Please."

He thrust forward immediately, and she moaned.

Summer couldn't believe the intense pleasure of his cock driving deep into her. Stretching her.

He'd said he needed her. That gave her a heady sense of control.

She clung to him, sucking in air.

"Please, fuck me, Master." The dirty erotic words aroused her to fever pitch.

"Yes, I'm going to fuck you hard and fast. You are going to come as soon as you feel me release."

"Yes, Master."

His cock drove deep.

"Oh, God, yes."

Deep and hard. She squeezed him inside her. His cock dragged against her insides as he thrust. In. Out. Harder. Faster.

Pleasure swept through her. She could feel him stiffen, his hard steel shaft deep inside her. Hot liquid erupted within her. She let go and blissful pleasure burst through every part of her, sweeping her away to a place of pure sensation, riding a wave of sound. A long, lingering moan.

"Ohhhhh, Master."

Summer awoke the next morning wrapped in Max's strong arms. She glanced up at him in wonder.

It had been an incredible night. A night of new experiences. New sensations.

After he'd finally made love to her, he'd dragged her off to bed and held her. All night long.

She smiled. She hadn't known what to expect of BDSM, but what Max had shown her had been . . . intensely sexy. She was thrilled she'd decided to stay last night.

A weekend fling. She was so happy Tanya had talked her into it.

She glanced at his handsome face, and a disturbing thought struck her. Would he want her for the whole weekend? Maybe he wanted just the one night. There were lots of sexy, willing women at Sex-à-la-Gala. Maybe he wanted variety.

"Good morning." Max's arms tightened around her.

Four

"Good morning." Summer hesitated. "Master."

She didn't know what the etiquette was. Did she stay in the submissive role?

He chuckled and flipped her onto her back, then prowled over her. His lips captured hers. His passionate kiss made her heart race.

"I hereby give you permission to *not* call me Master." He kissed her again, leaving her breathless. "Until tonight."

"Tonight?" She smiled. So he did want her again. In fact, by the feel of things, he wanted her now.

"That's right. I'm not going to let you get away that easily."

His hard cock slid across her belly, and she felt wetness ooze between her legs. He shifted his pelvis and his cock head nudged her slit, then slid right in. Deep. She gasped.

He kissed her neck and drew out his cock, then thrust in deep again.

"Oh, Max." She slid her hands over his shoulders and clung to him as he drove her pleasure higher with his thrusting cock. Plunging into her. Stretching her with his giant steel shaft.

"Yes." Heat rushed through her, flooding her with intense sensations. "I'm going to come."

He thrust harder and she gasped, then wailed in pure bliss. He groaned and followed her into orgasm.

Summer sat on the stool to give her feet a rest. There had been a steady stream of people passing by the booth this afternoon, many stopping to buy books. If she came back next year, she'd have to bring more chocolates.

"Hey, honey. Been busy while I was gone?" Tanya stepped through the gap between the tables and sat beside Summer on the second stool. She'd been in the workshop area doing another of her talks.

"Yes. You sold ten more books. Some people said they'd come back later to have you sign them."

"Great. Why don't you go take a break."

"Sounds like an excellent idea."

A tingle quivered down Summer's spine at the deep, masculine voice.

Max.

She glanced around and smiled at him. His six-foot-two-inch frame looked gorgeous in the black jeans and shirt he wore. Of course, he'd look gorgeous in anything. *And nothing.* He looked especially good in nothing.

"Summer, come with me."

She recognized the authority in his voice, and her body responded automatically. She stood up and grabbed her purse.

"Leave it here. You don't need it," he said.

She put it down and stepped out from behind the booth. "Are you hungry?"

"No, Tanya and I had a sandwich an hour ago."

He nodded, then led her down the corridor and into the hallway that led to the hotel next door. She followed him down the hall, then around a corner. It was quiet in this lower level to the lobby. He glanced around, then opened a door.

It was a single-person washroom. Nicely appointed, in keeping with an upscale hotel like this.

Max locked the door behind them.

"I have something for you." He handed her a package wrapped in black, glossy paper tied with a translucent neon green ribbon.

She took the package and pulled the ribbon to unfasten the bow. The ribbon fell free and she pulled open the wrapping on one end and tugged out the box. She opened it and found a small device amid the green neon tissue paper inside.

Max grinned and held out something in his hand.

"I can control it remotely." He flicked a button on the small control in his hand, which fit neatly within his palm, and the device in the box began to quiver.

Startled, she jerked back. My God, it was a vibrator. Small and silver.

"I can be thirty yards away, yet give you pleasure."

She had no doubt about that. He could look at her a certain way and she'd probably climax . . . with or without props.

He took the box from her hands and set it on the vanity.

"I want you to wear it this afternoon, and whenever I

want, I will turn it on. . . . I could make you come at any time."

The thought of the small device inside her . . . of him turning it on . . . or off . . . anytime he wanted, made her breath catch.

He stroked a hand over her shoulder, then down her back as he drew her closer. She could feel the heat radiating off his body. She wanted to step forward and press against him.

"I don't think it's a good idea." Some level of sanity pushed through her foggy brain.

"But you will wear it."

"I . . ." She should argue, but something stopped her.

He raised an eyebrow. "What is the correct response to a command?"

"Yes, Master." The words came automatically.

He smiled. "Good. Now, take off your top."

Her fingers flicked open the buttons of her blouse, slowly revealing her black lace bra beneath.

"You have beautiful tits, Summer." He turned her around to see herself in the mirror as she undressed. He stood behind her, his hot gaze admiring her body. "Do you like me calling them tits?"

"No." But in a way, she did. It made her feel dirty. And she liked it.

She dropped her shirt over her shoulders, and it slipped to the floor. His hands cupped her lace-covered breasts. The erotic sight of him stroking her breasts in the mirror sent her heartbeat thumping wildly. The feel of his hot, warm hands over her sent moisture pooling between her thighs.

"Now the bra. I want to see your tits naked, the nipples hard."

She reached around and unfastened the bra, then slid it off.

"Oh, yes. You have very beautiful tits."

Every time he said the word *tits,* it jarred her. It also made her intensely aware of her breasts and how the tight nipples jutted forward.

She gazed at his reflection in the mirror.

"Now stroke them."

She hesitated.

"Summer, stroke your breasts."

She ran her hand over one breast. The nipple spiked into her palm, aching to be toyed with. He grasped her shoulders and eased her backward, pressing her against his chest.

"Stroke the other one, too."

She cupped both of her breasts, then kneaded them lightly. Waves of heat washed through her.

"Tell me what you're doing."

"I'm caressing my . . . tits."

"Very good."

He turned her around and leaned toward her. His mouth surrounded one hard nipple, and he sucked it.

She moaned softly at the delicious heat thrumming through her.

"Now kneel on the floor in front of me." He leaned back against the vanity.

She knelt. She could see the bulge swelling in his pants.

"What do you say?"

"Yes, Master."

"Good. Do you know what I want you to do now?"

His erection pressed at his tight jeans.

"Yes, I think so, Master."

"Tell me."

"You want me to . . . perform oral sex."

"I want you to suck my cock. Say it."

"You want me to . . . suck your cock. Master."

"Very good."

She unfastened the snap on his black jeans, then drew down the zipper. His cock strained against his black briefs. She pushed his jeans down, then hooked her fingers in the waistband of the briefs and pulled them down. His lovely, long cock bobbed forward. She caught it in her hands. It was hot and hard. Her sex ached.

She leaned forward and licked the tip of him, then drew him into her mouth. He filled her with his massive girth. She licked him, then drew him deeper. He groaned. She licked and sucked. One hand glided around to his hard butt, and she stroked, then squeezed as she sucked him. She cupped his balls, fondling them while she bobbed up and down on his cock.

"Oh, baby, that's great."

His hand stroked over her breast, and she sucked him deep.

"I'm close. Suck me hard so I'll come."

She sucked and squeezed at the same time. He stiffened and . . . hot liquid filled her mouth.

"Swallow, Summer."

At his hoarse command, she did.

He drew free from her mouth.

"Lean back on the counter."

She stood up and leaned against the counter.

"Yes, Master."

He smiled as he lifted her onto the counter. He pushed up her skirt and reached underneath, then drew down her panties and tossed them aside.

"Spread your legs. Let me see that pretty little pussy of yours."

She opened her legs and he got on his knees, then leaned forward. His mouth connected with her hot, wet slit, and she thought she'd come on the spot. His tongue tunneled into her and licked. He nuzzled her clit, then swirled over it.

Oh, God, if he kept that up, she'd come any second. She just prayed he wouldn't tell her to hold off coming until he allowed it because . . . He sucked on her clit, and she moaned. She didn't think she'd be able to . . .

He drove two fingers into her and thrust them in and out while he licked and sucked her clit.

"Oh, yes." She clung to his head as the pleasure built to a crescendo.

"Tell me when you're coming, Summer."

"Yes, M—" Pleasure overwhelmed her and she gasped. "I'm coming . . . Master . . ."

She wailed as her nerve ends crackled with intense sensation. Then she gasped as bliss poured through her.

He drew his fingers free and stood up, smiling at her. She leaned back against the mirror, her legs still spread wide.

"Hmm. It's such a pretty pussy."

He lifted her from the counter and turned her to face the mirror.

"Lean over."

She leaned forward and he drew her skirt up over her

behind and stroked her buttocks. As she watched him in the mirror, she felt his hard cock press against the backs of her thighs, then he pushed inside. His tremendous length slid easily into her wet slit, and she groaned as he filled her up. He thrust deep, then drew back. She felt empty for a few seconds, then he thrust forward again. His hands wrapped around her hips, and he began to thrust in an even rhythm. Forward and back. Filling her, then withdrawing. An incredible heat built within her, then . . .

"I'm coming again. I'm . . ." She moaned. "Oh, yes. Master, I'm coming."

He thrust harder, then stiffened within her, and she could feel his hot liquid streaming inside her.

He held her tight to his body for a few moments, then he kissed the top of her head. They took a few moments to clean themselves up, but when she reached for her panties, he grabbed them and grinned.

"I think it's time to try on your gift."

He lifted her onto the vanity again.

"Open your legs."

She did so. Max lifted the small silver egg from the box, then she felt the cold metal against her wet flesh as he slid it inside.

Summer clenched her thighs together at the buzzing between her legs. Vibrant sensations quivered through her. Max had been teasing her on and off for the past hour, setting the little egg pulsing sometimes for a second or two, sometimes longer. Once he kept it going for about a minute and she thought she'd go over the edge, then he'd stopped.

The most exciting thing about this situation was Max's

total focus on her. He must constantly be thinking about her, watching her, enjoying his ability to give her pleasure.

The egg pulsed again, and she gritted her teeth. *If you can call this particular type of torment pleasure.*

She glanced around. She couldn't see him in the throng, but she had no doubt he was nearby. She could feel his hot gaze . . . and that excited her.

Her insides quivered with another vibration. Oh, man, she wanted more than a little device inside her right now.

"Excuse me."

Summer glanced up to see an attractive blond fellow on the other side of the table. He wore trendy jeans, a white shirt with a blue patterned tie, and a casual blazer.

"Yes, may I help you?" Summer smiled, hoping Max would refrain from his torment while she handled this customer.

"I hope so. I'm Kurt Jenson and I own three adult stores in the area. Are you the one who sells the chocolates?"

"Yes."

Music began to play from the big speakers by the stage, and Mistress Cassie went into her spiel. She said something about a contest, and people in the crowd around the stage cheered.

Kurt leaned forward and raised his voice over the noise. "Are you local?"

"No, I'm from Port Smith. I have a chocolate shop there."

"I'd love to carry your chocolates in my stores. The stores are aimed at couples . . . very high class."

A woman over a microphone started a loud moaning. Summer stared down the aisle at her partial view of the stage.

"It's a contest they're doing," Kurt explained. "The women pretend to orgasm."

Summer remembered they'd done the same thing last night. Woman after woman had taken her turn at the microphone, filling the large convention hall with the sound of orgasmic wails. As she shifted her gaze from the stage to the man in front of her, she felt her cheeks heat.

"I thought maybe we could meet for coffee tomorrow, before you head back home, and talk about details, if you're interested," he said.

Summer never would have guessed there'd be such a strong demand for chocolate penises. She didn't think she wanted to make them in the long run. It was fun this once, but she had a serious business to run.

"I . . . uh . . ." The egg started to quiver, and so did she. All thought of protest . . . or even what her name was . . . disappeared from her mind.

He offered her a black card. She hesitated, but the egg buzzed again and the woman onstage reached her peak and Summer couldn't help but notice how good Mr. Kurt Jenson looked in those tight jeans. Another woman took the microphone and started to moan. Summer took the card, and as her fingers brushed his, a sudden desire to drag the man behind the table and seriously molest him pulsed through her.

Another long, sexy moan.

Oh, God, if Max doesn't stop that, I'll make a total fool of myself.

"I'll stop by tomorrow." Kurt smiled and left unscathed.

"So, I see I have some competition," Max murmured from next to her ear.

Summer practically jumped at his sudden presence. She sent him a death stare, not in a mood to smooth his ruffled feathers after what he'd been putting her through. But he just smiled, obviously unconcerned.

Buzz . . . buzz . . .

Summer flopped onto her stool, fighting the intense urge to just let go and have an orgasm right here and now.

"I think you're enjoying my little gift. . . ."

She glared at him as his *gift* vibrated some more, making it difficult to suck in enough air.

"I think you'd enjoy it even more if you relaxed and let it do its job."

"I can't just . . . not here where everyone can see."

He nodded toward the stage. "Those women are."

Her eyes widened, knowing exactly what he was suggesting.

"Oh, no. No way."

The toy pulsed inside her, and she ached for release. The sound of the moaning woman in the background only made it worse.

"Tanya, don't you think Summer should give the contest a try?"

Tanya glanced up from her books, eyes twinkling. "Sounds like a great idea." An impish grin curled her lips. "Go for it, Summer."

"No, really . . ."

Pulse . . . pulse . . .

Traffic along the aisle in front of their table diminished as more people drifted toward the stage. A loud wail tore through the conference center from another contestant.

Tanya's eyes widened. "That sounds like a good one." She stood up. "I'm going over to watch. Want to join me?"

When Summer shook her head, Tanya glanced at Max. He slipped in behind the table and sat beside Summer.

"I think I'll stay here and keep Summer company."

Tanya shrugged. "Okay. Have fun, you two." She strolled down the aisle toward the throng of people around the stage.

Another woman started gasping onstage. Max slid his arm around Summer's waist.

"It really sounds like she's coming, doesn't it?" He smiled at Summer as the device pulsed inside her again.

"Uh-huh," was all she could manage to say as she gazed into his ember-hot eyes.

"I think you're close." He drew her tighter to his side. "I think you could come right now."

Five

Summer's fingers clenched around the edge of the table.

Then the egg began to vibrate again. The vibrating turned to a pulsing. And it didn't stop. She felt her knees go rubbery.

Her stomach tightened and she moaned, then quickly glanced around to see if anyone had noticed. There was no one visible except the woman at the next booth, and she had her back to them as she reorganized her stock. Not that she could have heard Summer over the din of the moaning woman at the microphone.

The pulsing jumped up a notch. Summer had to stifle another moan. She flattened her palm on the table as she sucked in air.

Her insides throbbed with need. He increased the intensity again. She dragged her hand over her hair as pleasure washed through her . . . sweeping away her inhibitions.

She focused on Max's lips, wanting them on her clit. Wanting him to make her . . .

"Ohhhh . . . ," she murmured, trying to stifle the sound. The pulsing increased . . . surely at the max now. . . .

"You're close, aren't you." He grinned broadly. "Just think of my hands stroking your breasts," he murmured in her ear.

Her nipples throbbed.

"Of me licking your sweet little clit."

Buzz . . . buzz . . .

Oh, man, she wanted it bad.

Pulse . . . pulse . . .

Max nuzzled her ear. "Come, sweetheart."

Her body responded to his command. Waves of intense sensations rose through her and washed her insides with throbbing pleasure.

She wanted to scream out loud. She clutched her head as the pleasure catapulted her to a blossoming, mind-numbing orgasm, made all the more potent because she was trying to hold it in.

"I think we have a winner," said a voice over the microphone.

Summer's eyelids snapped open . . . she hadn't realized she'd closed them.

Max chuckled. "She wasn't talking about you, sweetheart. Although your orgasm *was* spectacular, I'm the only one who witnessed it."

Then he kissed her. His lips caressed hers with a gentle passion that took her breath away. She melted against him, her arms gliding around his neck.

"Hey, you two. Look what I got."

Summer glanced around to see Tanya waltzing behind the table, flicking her finger under a glittering pendant hanging on a chain around her neck. It was a two-inch number sign symbol followed by the digit 1, all in rhinestones.

"You entered the contest?" Summer asked.

Tanya grinned broadly. "Yes, I did. And I scored the big prize."

Summer just grinned at her as she squeezed Max's hand. *That's what she thinks.*

"I think Max is good for you, Summer," Tanya said as she sipped her coffee in the little café about two blocks from the hotel. "He's really helping you open up."

Max had offered to watch the booth so Tanya and Summer could get away from the conference hall and have a proper break, rather than a quick coffee to go.

"I worry about you sometimes, honey. You don't date. You're pining after two of your closest friends and you won't go after either of them . . . and all you do is work. You deserve someone to make you happy."

"It's not like Max and I are going to become a couple or anything. This is just for the weekend."

Tanya nodded. "I guess so. Long-distance romances are pretty tough."

There was more distance between Summer and Max than miles. He led a totally different life. He lived in New York City and ran some kind of big high-tech firm, whereas Summer lived in a small town and owned a small shop making chocolates. There was no way Max would want her lifestyle . . . and she wouldn't leave Port Smith. She loved it there. It was her home.

Max was a powerful man—in business and in his sexual life. He was a Dominant. Although she could enjoy the submissive role for a weekend fling, she didn't think she'd want to do it as part of a long-term thing.

Still, being dominated by Max was hotter than hell. She wondered if she'd ever be satisfied with regular vanilla sex again.

"I have something for you." Max handed Summer a large gift-wrapped box with a big red bow.

The show had closed for the evening about a half hour ago, and Max had escorted Summer to his suite. She pulled off the ribbon and discarded it, then opened the box. A hot pink shoebox sat nestled in black tissue, along with three smaller boxes. She opened the shoebox, and inside were the gorgeous black shoes she'd seen at the show yesterday. She lifted one in her hand, and the slender silver stiletto heel gleamed in the light.

"Thank you! Oh, Max, I can't believe you went back and bought them for me." She pulled on the shoe and fastened the strap, then tilted her foot back and forth, admiring it. "They're so sexy."

She put on the other one, then lifted the smallest box from the tissue. She opened it to find a lovely necklace with a large rhinestone "S" on a silver chain.

"It's very pretty."

"It doesn't stand for Summer." His eyes glinted as he smiled at her. "It stands for slave."

"Oh."

She held the "S" in the palm of her hand, watching it glitter in the light, and realized it would be a wonderful souvenir of this weekend. When she wore it, everyone would assume it was her initial, but she would know differently, so it would always remind her of Max and their exciting time together.

"I want you to wear these gifts tonight."

"I'd love to." She held up the necklace. "Would you put it on for me?"

She turned her back to him and held up her hair. As his fingers played along the back of her neck, sending tingles down her spine, the "S" dropped beneath her camisole top and nestled between her breasts.

Max slid his finger under the silver chain at her collarbone, then glided down to the neckline of her top. He drew up the chain until the pendant reappeared.

"Very nice, but I meant I want you to wear *just* the gifts."

"Oh." She glanced inside the big box. "Those too?"

He smiled and nodded.

There were two gifts left, but judging from the size of the boxes, whatever items were in them were tiny.

She opened the bigger box to find long black satin gloves. As soon as she opened the other, she saw the glint of rhinestones again . . . this time as a decoration on the tops of black stockings—the type with elastic at the top so they'd stay up without garters. Each had three rhinestones set close together as a small decoration on the top band.

This was all he wanted her to wear? Her cheeks warmed—as much in eager anticipation as in embarrassment. She gathered the boxes and stood up, but as she took a couple of steps toward the bedroom to change, Max stopped her.

"Where are you going?"

"To the bedroom to change."

"No."

She locked gazes with him. "No?"

"I want you to change right here."

Oh, my.

She placed the boxes on the table, then self-consciously lifted the hem of her camisole top. Hesitating, she glanced at Max as he watched her with great interest.

She pulled off her top, then unfastened her black satin bra and dropped it on the table. Her nipples grew rigid immediately, more from Max's intent gaze than the coolness of the air.

"Keep going," Max commanded.

She sat and unfastened the straps of the sexy high-heeled shoes and kicked them off, then stood up and shed her pants. Next, she pushed her panties down and stepped out of them. She now stood naked in front of him, except for the slave pendant between her breasts.

Max handed her the stockings, and she sat down and drew on one, then the other. She stepped back into the shoes and fastened the ankle straps, then stood up. She drew on each glove, slowly and purposefully, paying close attention to drawing each finger carefully into place, enjoying Max's gaze warming her body.

Oh, God, she felt sexy standing here with her arms and legs clothed and her torso totally naked. Her breasts felt heavy and swollen with need and . . . she was very conscious of her upper thighs and . . . everything—especially with Max's gaze focused . . . right there.

"Perfect." He stood up and opened the closet by the door, then returned with a black coat, which he held up. "Now put this on."

Her eyebrows furrowed, but she slid her arms into the sleeves as he held the coat for her, then tied the belt at the waist. Why would he want her to be practically naked, then cover herself with a coat?

"Now these."

He handed her some sunglasses. When she placed them on her face, she found that the lenses were totally black, and they were cushioned inside so they sat snugly around her eyes. She couldn't see a thing.

"Now come with me."

He took her elbow and led her forward. She heard the door open and realized he was leading her into the hallway. Where was he taking her?

They turned right, walked a ways, then turned left. It was very strange walking around in total blackness, her only assurance that she wouldn't walk into a wall Max's hand guiding her by the arm.

After a few moments, they stopped. She was pretty sure they were at the elevator. A ding confirmed it. She could hear the doors whoosh open, then Max eased her forward. He turned her around, and the doors closed. Were there other people in the elevator with them? She didn't think so.

She felt the elevator start moving, then slow down. A ding sounded again and the doors opened. The hum of voices surrounded her as they stepped out of the elevator. The lobby. She could feel the hard floor beneath her feet as they walked and hear the clacking sound of her heels on the marble, different from the carpeted hallway upstairs.

"Wait while I get the door," Max murmured against her ear as he slowed his pace. They stopped, then he pressed his hand to her back and eased her forward again. The lobby sounds muted behind them, but she could tell they hadn't stepped outside. There were no traffic sounds, and the air did not carry the fresh scent of the flowers from the garden at the front of the hotel. They continued forward, went through another door, then walked for five more minutes or so.

Finally, they came to a halt.

"We're here. Now, Summer, take off the coat."

Goose bumps quivered across her arms. She had no idea where they were. No idea if there were people around. And it felt as though they were somewhere fairly open.

She hesitated. Could she really take off her coat, leaving herself naked for who knew who to see?

"Summer, take off the coat."

Could she do this? Her safe word—cat—quivered on her tongue.

"Obey me, Summer. Show me how much you trust me."

She did trust him. She didn't know why, since she'd known him not much more thans a day, but deep down she trusted him—and she wanted to obey him.

She unfastened the tie at her waist and opened her coat, then dropped it to the floor. Cool air washed over her skin. Her nipples puckered. She heard a metallic clang, then felt Max's hands on her arms as he eased her backward. She stopped at the feel of cold metal against her backside, then another clang. She moved her arms a little to the side and banged against metal. Bars. She tried moving her arms forward . . . and hit metal bars again.

"You're in a cage."

She felt Max's fingers brush along her temple, then the dark glasses were pulled from her face. She blinked a few times and gazed at bars just a few inches in front of her face. This was not a large rectangular cage that gave her room to move around. It was tall enough for her to stand inside but only slightly wider than her shoulders, and the depth barely gave her room to breathe.

A stifling sense of confinement sucked the breath from her, but she stared past the bars, assuring herself that if she wanted out of the cage, Max would let her out. The sense of openness in the large space beyond the cage settled her nerves yet at the same time made her feel exposed.

Various pieces of strange but familiar furniture surrounded her. This was the dungeon that had been set up at the convention center. Red curtains vaguely defined the space and blocked her view of most of the booths beyond, with an opening of about ten feet wide where convention visitors could walk in and out of the space.

"I pulled some strings and arranged for us to have exclusive use of the dungeon this evening."

The show was closed for the night, so no one was around. But there could be cleaning staff . . . security guards . . . curious visitors.

"Don't worry. The place is locked up. We're completely alone."

He smiled as he walked by the cage, then around behind her. With her attire . . . or lack thereof . . . and the way the cage held her in place . . . she couldn't stop him from looking at her. Not that she wanted to.

She couldn't see Max, but she could feel his presence . . . then she felt his hand stroke along her back, then over her buttocks. Another hand stroked around and cupped her breast. He stroked around and around the nipple, sending her hormones into a flutter.

His hands slipped away and he stepped in front of her again. Slowly, he began to remove his clothes. He started with his shirt, unfastening each button purposefully, his gaze locked on her body . . . shifting from the tips of her breasts to her naked thighs and the private juncture above. . . .

She watched as he revealed his muscular chest . . . one button at a time. He slid the garment from his strong shoulders and tossed it aside. Her gaze lingered on his sculpted, rock-hard abs as he unfastened his belt. He unzipped his black pants and dropped them to the ground, then kicked them aside. His cock strained at his black briefs.

She shifted in the cage, intensely aware of how limited her movement was. He peeled off his briefs, and she licked her lips at the sight of his enormous, stiff cock. He stepped toward her.

"Lean forward. Against the cage," he instructed.

As she did, the cold metal bars striped her skin. The tips of her breasts pushed through the three-inch spaces between the bars. Max ran his fingers over the cage, petting her nipples with soft strokes. Pleasure melted through her, and she wanted to feel his hands on more of her. He leaned down and licked one nipple, then drew it into his mouth. She arched against the cage. Moisture pooled between her thighs. She yearned to feel him inside her.

He stood up and nuzzled her cheek, which pressed tight against the bars. The tip of his cock pushed through the bars and brushed her thighs. He wrapped one hand around his shaft and guided his cock over her thighs, then pressed it between her legs. It stroked along her slit to her ass. She clenched, grasping him firmly between her thighs, wishing he'd push right inside her. He shifted forward and back, stroking her wet, aching slit.

She heard a sound, like a door closing, then footsteps.

Oh, God, someone will see me. Will see what we're doing.

Max stepped back.

"Don't worry." He quickly donned his pants and disappeared around the curtain.

She heard Max's voice and a quiet discussion. A few moments later, footsteps receded and a door closed again. Max returned.

"It was the security guard. I explained the arrangement I made for this evening and he left." He smiled. "Don't worry. No details."

He dropped his pants to the ground again and stepped toward her.

Summer's hands were quivering, and she sucked in a deep breath. He stroked up and down her back. Relaxing her. Soothing her.

Soon anxiety turned to anticipation. He stepped behind the cage and his hands slipped between the bars and glided over her breasts, then he drew her back against the cold, hard bars. She became intensely aware of his warm, hard chest pressing against her between those bars, his large hands encompassing her breasts . . . and his steel-hard cock pressing against her backside.

His hands stroked down her naked body, over her hips, then around her rib cage. He cupped her breasts again and massaged her soft flesh with firm, sure fingers. Her nipples ached and she sucked in deeper breaths.

One of his hands moved to her neck, then his fingers traced her jaw. He drew her head back against the cage and nuzzled her ear.

"You are completely helpless to me right now. Do you know that?"

"Yes, Master."

His hand fell from her breast and she felt the tip of his steel-hard cock glide against her buttocks, then slip between her thighs. He glided forward and back, stroking her wet slit, making her melt more liquid heat.

Would he impale her from behind? Drive into her while she stood helpless in this cage?

She wanted to lean forward in invitation, but the confining cage would not allow her to.

His hot shaft drew away, and a moment later he appeared in front of the cage, pushing a wooden stairway with three steps. He walked up the steps and stood in front of her, his delicious cock pointing straight toward her, and at the perfect height.

He pressed his cock head to her lips and she sucked him inside, reveling at the feel of his bulbous head filling her mouth. She licked the tip, then swirled her tongue around him. He pushed deeper, and she opened as wide as she could to accommodate his breadth. She sucked and pulsed her mouth around him. He tucked his hands around her head and stroked her hair as he thrust in and out of her mouth.

She loved his big, hard cock gliding into her. He tensed, and she knew he would climax soon . . . but he surprised her by drawing himself free, then pressing his cock tight against his body. She leaned forward and licked his balls, then wrapped her lips around one and drew it inside. She pulsed it gently in her mouth, then released it and drew in the other. He groaned, then drew back again.

Had she displeased him?

He stepped down from the stairway and pushed it out of the way, then unlocked the cage.

"Come over here."

She could read nothing from his voice. He took her arm and drew her toward an interesting contraption that consisted of a padded leather bench with padded supports for her knees, shoulders, and arms.

"Kneel on the pads and lean over."

She knelt on the knee pads, which were long enough to support her from knee to ankle, then draped her body over the padded bench. Her head hung over the edge, but her shoulders and elbows rested against padding. With her ass pushed high and fully exposed, she wondered if he was going to punish her. She dampened even more at the thought.

Max grasped her ankle and she felt a strap wrap around it, pulling her ankle snug against the padding. He fastened her other ankle, then fastened straps just below her knees.

"What a lovely view," he said, then fastened a strap around her waist.

A moment later, he stepped in front of her and fastened first one wrist, then the other into place in front of her. Her back end was totally accessible . . . to see or touch . . . and she couldn't do a thing about it.

"How does that feel, Summer? Do you like being my prisoner?"

A deep yearning flooded her . . . to have Max touch her . . . to press his fingers into her . . . for that sturdy, enormous cock of his to plunge deep inside her.

"Yes, Master."

"What do you like about it?"

"I . . . uh . . . like that you're looking at me."

"I *like* looking at you. What else?"

"I like that . . . you can touch me."

His fingers stroked over the top curve of her buttocks, then slowly stroked downward.

"Yes, I can. And I *love* touching you. What else?"

"I . . . like . . . submitting to you."

He stroked her behind, then down her inner thigh, then up the other one, skimming past her private flesh.

"Hmm. Yes." He moved behind her. "Do you like being vulnerable to me?"

His finger stroked lightly over her slit. At the sudden contact, her knees jerked together . . . at least they tried to, but the straps held them firm. She could do nothing to stop his access to her . . . which made her ache for him all the more.

His fingers, now slick from her juices, glided upward, and he slid one finger into her back opening. His other fingers teased the outside while the first slid in deep, rocking back and forth.

Then his fingers slipped away.

She almost jumped at the sudden, and quite erotic, feel of his lips on her lower back. He glided down the curve of her ass, then his mouth covered her wet slit and he teased her delicate flesh with his tongue. She moaned at the exquisite sensation.

A sound in the distance startled her, and she jerked again. Could the guard be coming back?

Max positioned his head between her spread legs and licked her, then pressed his tongue inside and stroked. The band around her waist prevented her from arching, but she managed to push a little against him, giving his tongue access to delve a little deeper. Then he licked her clit. She moaned, then the sound deepened as he fluttered his tongue over her bud, then sucked it. His hands stroked over her ass as he toyed with her. Pleasure swelled inside her and burst through her cells like a supernova. She wailed in sheer delight as an orgasm blasted through her.

"You are so fucking sexy," he murmured.

Hard flesh nudged against her opening from behind, and his enormous cock thrust into her, stretching her with its girth. Her spasms of pleasure increased. He drew back and thrust forward again . . . and again. His thrusting sped up until he pounded into her in a steady rhythm.

Her pleasure built again, rising . . . propelling her to a blissful state.

"Oh, yes, Master." She sucked in a breath, then wailed in ecstatic release.

His hands tightened around her hips as he thrust more slowly but deeper, then he stiffened against her as his cock erupted inside her.

He pressed his chest against her back, not resting his full weight on her but holding her against him in a cuddle of sorts. He nuzzled her ear.

"You are a gem."

After a few moments, he unfastened the strap around her waist, then the ones around her calves and ankles. A moment later, he freed her wrists and helped her up. He drew her into his arms and held her against his body and stroked her hair. His closeness and his gentle touch made her feel loved and cared for.

As much as she wanted to grab her coat and tug it on in case a guard came around the curtain, she did not want to interrupt this perfect moment.

He tucked his finger under the "S" pendant and lifted it.

"You are the perfect slave. I'll really miss you when you leave tomorrow."

Her chest tightened. Tomorrow she would return to Port Smith, and Max would return to New York. She'd never see him again.

Of course that's what she'd wanted, right? A weekend fling with no lingering attachments?

Now, however, the realization that she would never see Max again crept through her with a stinging sorrow. She didn't want to give him up. He'd opened her to new experiences . . . to a new level of pleasure.

Although she and Max would never make sense as a long-term relationship, it didn't mean they couldn't enjoy a blazing hot, short-term fling. If only they lived closer together. If only Max wanted to see her again.

But surely he was just being polite. Saying what lovers say after an incredible coupling.

She just had to face the fact that tomorrow meant goodbye.

Six

Tanya handed Summer the display stand she'd used for the cocksuckers, and Summer placed it in the cardboard box along with her tabletop signs.

"I think that's it," Tanya said.

Summer surveyed the booth. Both tables were totally clear. Tanya's boxes sat on the floor at the end of the table, all packed and ready to go. Summer shifted the rented chairs under the table and glanced around, checking for any little thing she might have forgotten, but she knew deep inside she was just stalling because she did not want to say goodbye to her friend.

Or Max.

She glanced down at the rhinestone "S" that sparkled on the backdrop of her black T-shirt. Her fingers stroked over the bumpy surface.

Max had invited her to join him for dinner, but she wanted to get home before dark. Everything about the show had been exhilarating, but exhausting—including her experience with Max—so she didn't want to push herself. The drive back to Port Smith would take at least two hours, and it was already six-thirty.

"All set?" Max asked.

She nodded, and he picked up the cardboard box and set it on the trolley they'd borrowed, then he placed Tanya's boxes beside Summer's. They'd already put their suitcases in the car that morning when they'd checked out before the show.

"I'll take these out to the cars and give you two time to say good-bye," Max said as he pulled the trolley away.

Tanya threw her arms around Summer. "I'm going to miss you. We really should do this more often." She leaned in and whispered in Summer's ear, "And you should really do Max more often."

"We were just a weekend fling, remember? No one at home will ever know about it."

"Yeah? You're not even going to tell Kyle and Shane about it?"

Especially not Kyle and Shane.

But Summer said nothing.

"Max has been good for you. I wish the two of you could keep going."

"Tanya, you know that won't work. We live too far away, for one thing."

"And I bet you have a million other reasons, too. Right?"

Summer just shrugged.

Tanya grabbed her purse from the floor and started walking, and Summer fell into step beside her. "At least tell me you're going to do something about Kyle and Shane."

"What do you mean, 'do something'?"

Tanya nudged her arm. "You know what I mean. You've had the hots for both of them for a long time. You just have to make your move."

"I don't have any moves."

"Oh, I'm sure Max has taught you some." She grinned impishly. "Seriously, though. Just let them know you're interested. You can't want to go back to just mooning over them and wishing. Make it happen. Take a chance."

"Well, it would be a lot easier if I could decide which one to go for."

"Which one do you want more?"

"I don't know. I like them in different ways."

"Then go after them both."

Summer rolled her eyes. "Tanya, stop worrying about me, okay?"

"But I do. I worry you'll die an old maid still wishing you could get into those two handsome hunks' pants. And they're just as bad." She nudged Summer again. "Just do it!"

"Do what?" Max glanced at them as they approached the two cars—Tanya's and Summer's—parked side by side.

"Seduce the two guys she has the hots for back home."

"Tanya!"

"Oh, don't worry, Summer. Max is a man of the world."

"I agree with Tanya. If you want these men, go after them." He placed his hands on her shoulders and drew her close for a quick kiss, then smiled. "Or do I have to order you to do it?"

"You know, that's probably the only thing that would work." Tanya grinned.

Summer wanted to respond, but this close to Max she

felt breathless. No words would come. Max captured her lips for a deep, passionate kiss, and she forgot all about Tanya and her teasing—thinking only of Max.

And Summer kept thinking of Max. All the way home. Then all night long, until she fell asleep. Then she dreamed of Max. And chains. And a huge, rigid cock that pulsed and pleasured her until she screamed in release. She awoke the next morning with the sheets tangled around her legs and an orgasm still pulsing through her.

Good heavens, she'd never had such a powerfully erotic dream before. And she'd certainly never actually come to climax before.

The sun peeked through her curtains, and she glanced at her clock. Seven forty-nine. Eleven minutes before her alarm would go off.

She lay back in bed and realized it was time to let go of thoughts of Max. Soon she'd be at work, and Shane and Kyle would ask her about the show. They'd tease her and they'd laugh and chat.

And she'd be totally aware of their masculinity . . . and her intense attraction to them . . . because Max had reminded her how sensual she could be. And how very much she liked sex.

She doubted she could go back to being just friends with Shane and Kyle again.

And that presented quite a problem.

Summer opened the box from her favorite candy supplier and stared at the lovely assortment of new chocolate molds. The heart-shaped box with a bow on top would be a delightful addition to her inventory. People loved boxes made of chocolate, especially when she filled them with small jelly candies.

The bell over the door tinkled.

"Hey, stranger, nice to have you back."

She twirled around and smiled at Shane. "Nice to be back."

At least it was now that she saw Shane's handsome smiling face. Last night, lying in bed with moonlight casting a glow across her white bedspread, she'd desperately wished that she were back in Chicago—in Max's arms.

She gazed at Shane affectionately. He had a cop's build, tall and broad-shouldered, but he'd left the force a couple of years ago to start his own security company. Since then, he'd grown his wavy blond hair to his shoulders, and he smiled a lot more. He was too much of a free spirit to thrive in the regimented environment of the police force.

As she drank in the sight of his broad smile and dazzling blue eyes, she wondered if she might really be able to change her relationship with Shane to a romantic one.

Or with Kyle.

Why not go out with both? Max's words echoed through her mind. *I mean have a threesome. Then you don't have to choose.*

After what she'd experienced this weekend, the thought of a threesome shouldn't intimidate her, but . . . it did. Anyway, she intended to leave the wild and sexually uninhibited woman she'd become back in Chicago.

"So, you ready for coffee?" he asked.

She turned around and grabbed her purse from the lower cabinet, then spun around and stepped from behind the counter. Was it just her imagination, or was he actually checking her out? And with a disturbingly hungry gaze?

It must be an aftereffect of the hormone rush from being with Max.

"Cindy, I'm gone for coffee. Be back in twenty minutes," she called. "I'll bring you one back."

"Okay," Cindy responded from the office. "Take your time."

This was their usual routine. Cindy liked to read her e-mail while she drank her coffee rather than go down to the coffee shop.

Shane opened the door for Summer, and they walked across the lobby of the hotel that housed Summer's chocolate shop. They made their way to the restaurant in the corner and sat at their usual table overlooking the river. It was quiet this time of the morning, with only two other couples in the restaurant.

"Usual?" asked Carol, the friendly, momlike waitress.

Summer and Shane both nodded. Carol poured coffee into the cups sitting on the table, then returned a few moments later with a banana-nut muffin for Summer and a Western sandwich for Shane.

"So, how was the trade show?" Shane grinned.

At least he'd stopped calling it the sex trade show. She'd felt as though she were going off to a hookers convention when he'd said that.

"It was . . . interesting." To say the least.

"See any naked people?"

She felt her cheeks heat as she thought of pony-girl. Shane had teased her mercilessly before she'd left because she'd been concerned about exactly that . . . seeing naked people at the show. When she'd decided to make the chocolate penises, she'd done it after hours because if Shane had found out, she'd never have lived it down.

"You *did*." Shane chuckled.

"Did what?" Kyle pulled back a chair and sat down.

His wavy medium brown hair, cropped short on the sides but longer on top, glistened with highlights from the time he spent in the sun by his backyard pool and the walks he took every lunch hour.

"Summer saw naked people at the show."

He gazed at her with his intense sea green eyes as he leaned forward, one eyebrow raised. "You had a pretty wild time, I take it?"

Her face flushed hotter. His tone was light, but the tight set of his square jaw told her he was concerned. When he looked at her like that, she could see a little of his admiral father in him.

Carol appeared with a coffeepot in hand, and Kyle nodded. Whenever he joined them for a break, he had time for only a quick coffee. Managing the hotel kept him pretty busy. He thanked her as she went on her way, efficient as always.

"Tell us about it." Kyle spooned some sugar into his coffee, then stirred.

Shane chuckled and sat back in his chair. "Especially the naked people."

"Well, there was this woman . . . with a harness of sorts . . . and a feather on top of her head. She was sort of like . . . a pony."

"This harness didn't cover much, I take it." Shane took a bite of his sandwich.

"Not really."

"Was the whole show like that?" Kyle asked, then sipped his coffee.

"The only nudity was the pony-girl."

"What else went on there?" Kyle asked.

She glanced at him. Could he tell she'd had a romantic entanglement with someone?

Her fingers wandered to the pendant hanging around her neck and stroked over the rhinestone "S."

Romantic? Who was she kidding? Breathtaking, exciting, wildly erotic. Yes. *Romantic*? No.

Guilt washed through her at the memory of what she'd done with Max. She felt as though she'd cheated on Kyle and Shane. Which was totally ridiculous, since the relationship she'd always had with both of them was merely friendship, no matter how much she'd longed for it to be more.

Shane rested his chin on his hand. "Yes, tell us what goes on at a sex trade show."

"There were a lot of booths with adult toys, lingerie, some information booths, and . . . they had a dungeon set up."

At the memory of what she and Max had shared in that dungeon—which sent her body into a flutter of need—she wished she hadn't mentioned that last part.

"Chains, whips, that sort of thing?" Kyle asked.

She nodded. "And a cage just big enough for a person to stand in."

Just the memory of being locked in that cage, with Max touching her naked body, sent heat flooding through her.

She stroked her pendant.

"Tell us about the stage shows," Shane said.

"Oh, I was too busy at the booth to watch them."

Of course, she wouldn't tell them how she'd participated. At the thought of the chocolate penis incident, heat
washed across her cheeks.

And there was no way on God's green earth she would
tell them about the orgasm contest. Shane would insist she
tell them all about it, and Kyle would be totally disap-
proving. One of them would pick up on her discomfort
because of what had happened at the table while the contest
was going on . . . how she had . . .

Thinking about the little egg vibrating inside her . . .
how turned on she'd been . . . while sitting with Shane and
Kyle . . . Suddenly, she became very aware of their masculinity. Their strong hands. Their sensual mouths.

She took a sip of her coffee and realized she'd finished
the cup and somewhere along the way she'd nibbled the
muffin to completion, too. She glanced at her watch.

"I really have to be getting back. My new molds came
today and I want to try them out."

Kyle glanced at Shane, giving him the *Let's stay and talk*
glance.

"You go ahead. I'm going to finish my coffee," Kyle
said.

Summer stood up and headed for the door. As Kyle
watched her, he ached inside. He'd wanted her for so long.
He glanced at Shane, knowing his friend felt the same
about her. It was a bit of a mess and kept both of them
hanging on the sidelines. Wanting Summer but not doing
anything about it.

"She was with someone," Kyle said.

Shane glanced at him. "She was with Tanya."

"Don't play dumb. You know what I mean. She met a man. Had sex. Who knows what kind of kinky, strange sex, too."

"Summer? No way." Shane glanced toward the door she'd exited just a few seconds earlier. "Well, maybe the sex part, but not the kinky stuff."

"Oh, yeah? Did you notice how many times she blushed?"

Summer finished dinner and put her dishes in the dishwasher, then relaxed on the couch with a book. She glanced out her window at the sky ablaze in sunset and the mature trees in her backyard, allowing her privacy from the neighboring houses.

It was nice being home, and it had been good seeing Shane and Kyle today. Great, in fact. A deep yearning quivered through her. Over the weekend, Max had distracted her with his powerful magnetism, but seeing Shane and Kyle today had reminded her why she'd been hung up on them for so long.

The phone rang, and she picked up the cordless handset on the side table next to her.

"Hello?"

"Hello, Summer."

Summer almost dropped the phone at the sound of Max's voice.

Seven

Max sat back in his office chair and put his feet up on his desk, thoroughly relaxed.

"Miss me?"

"Yes . . ." She hesitated, and Max could tell she'd almost said "Master."

"I've missed you, too."

And he had. Especially her sweetness and her delightful submissiveness.

He never allowed himself to get too attached to his subs, but when he parted with one, he always left her happier. Not because of the mutually satisfying sex, but because he helped her grow as a person.

While training a sub, he learned a lot about her personality, and he had a natural talent for figuring out what issues prevented her from achieving what she wanted at this stage in her life. He suspected he'd inherited his intuition from his mother, whom people were always turning to for help. Growing up, he had never appreciated what a wonderful gift it was. Until that horrible day . . .

His heart clenched at the memory of the call telling him

that Elena, his beloved wife of four years, the woman he had wanted to grow old with, had died in a car crash.

On that day, his life had changed. He'd thrown himself into his work to the exclusion of all else. He would have become a machine, like the high-tech toys he designed, without an ounce of humanity in his life, if it hadn't been for his mother. She'd coaxed him back from the abyss, convincing him the world was a place worth savoring rather than hiding from. Mom's gentle nature and loving concern as she helped him through that agonizing time had made him realize what a wonderful thing it was to help another human being, especially in such a personal way.

He knew no woman would ever touch his heart like Elena, but that didn't mean he couldn't allow women into his life. It would just be on his terms, and being a Dom ensured that. It also helped him to push a woman past her issues so he could help her achieve greater happiness.

After Summer left Chicago, he realized that he hadn't done as much for her as he could have. He had opened her to new ideas and helped her past her initial inhibitions, but she wasn't ready to embrace what she really wanted. She held herself back in life and in love, afraid to take risks. Tanya confirmed his theory when she told him Summer tended to do what was easy for her and what she knew would be successful. She did run her own business, but with modest results. With her talent, she could be staggeringly successful. With her sensual nature, she could have a rich and rewarding love life. But even with two men interested in her, she remained frozen in a friendship that she wished were more. And he knew that wouldn't change. When she'd said goodbye to Max, she'd also said good-bye to the intrepid explorer she'd become while away from her everyday world. She'd done well on their erotic weekend of discovery to push past the limits she generally set, but only because she'd taken that first step in giving up control. And Max wanted to help her continue on her path.

"Just because we aren't in the same city doesn't mean we can't interact in . . . interesting ways."

"What kind of ways?"

"Are you wearing the necklace I gave you?"

"Yes."

"What about the shoes?"

She hesitated. "As a matter of fact, I am. And nothing else."

He grinned. "Wonderful."

When Summer awoke the next morning, she still felt hot and needy. During her phone call with Max last night, she had used a new vibrator she'd bought at the show, and Max had talked her through a sensational erotic fantasy, sending her into a shattering orgasm. But sex with a machine, even with Max's sexy voice enhancing the experience, wasn't the same as sex with a live, hot-blooded man.

She went to work, still yearning for a man's touch. The longing haunted her as she handled the morning sales. When Shane showed up for their coffee break, she was ready for more than coffee. She sat at the table, and Shane chatted with her about the new security system Kyle intended to install in the hotel. Since Shane had left the police force and started his own security company, the hotel had become one of his main clients. He spent mornings and a couple of afternoons a week there, handling security issues, managing the security guards who worked at the hotel, and doing long-range planning.

A sound interrupted their conversation. Summer stared at her purse, which was sitting on the chair beside her, a persistent melody emanating from it.

"Your purse is ringing," Shane said.

She unsnapped the purse, then opened the small zippered compartment and pulled out the phone.

"Hello, Summer."

"Hi." A tingle skittered down her spine at the sound of Max's deep, sexy voice.

"Did I catch you at a bad time?"

"Um . . . I'm just at coffee break with a friend."

"Kyle or Shane?"

She glanced sidelong at Shane, then at her coffee cup. "Yes. My friend Shane."

"What about Kyle?"

"No, not today." She knew her voice sounded stilted, but she felt uncomfortable talking to Max—her recent lover—in front of Shane.

"All right. I don't want to interrupt. I'll call you this afternoon."

"Okay, good-bye."

"Who was that?" Shane sipped his coffee.

"Oh, just someone I met at the show."

"Really? A male someone?"

She hesitated. "Yes. He was a friend of Tanya's."

Shane sipped his coffee, seemingly relaxed, but she could sense the tension in him. His gaze rested on her as though he were trying to assess her feelings.

"Did you . . . have sex with him?"

Her stomach knotted, and she stared at him. It wasn't like Shane to ask about her sex life. Of course, over the past year she hadn't really had a sex life. Not while caught up in her desire for both Kyle and Shane and not knowing what to do about it.

"Yes."

Shane's gaze bored into her. His fingers, which were wrapped around his cup, gripped it tighter.

"Why? What was special about him?"

She took a sip of her coffee. "Well, uh . . . he was tall and sexy and . . . different."

"In what way?"

"I don't know . . . kind of . . . big city. Mysterious . . ." She sipped her coffee again, gripping her cup with both hands. "Commanding."

She wasn't sure why she'd said it. She knew Shane would probably delve deeper. And maybe she wanted him to. Maybe she wanted to admit how much being dominated had turned her on.

Shane pushed aside his coffee cup. "I have to go round to catering. Why don't you walk with me?"

He tossed some money on the table to cover their bill, even though it was Summer's turn, then stood up and walked toward the door. Summer grabbed her purse and followed him. Once in the lobby, he turned right immediately, down the corridor to catering, but then strode past the catering office to a quiet corridor that rarely had any traffic this time of the morning.

He drew her around a corner and stopped.

"Shane, what's going on?"

"Did you get into some kinky stuff with this guy?"

"Not kinky." She drew in a deep breath. "Domination and submission is not kinky. It's a willing exchange of power."

Erotic sensations washed through her as she remembered Max's authoritative voice commanding her to do sexy things.

"So this guy told you what to do. Did he tie you up?"

She remembered how Max had strapped her to that bench, leaving her helpless against his touch. How he had stroked her . . . how he had slid his big cock into her . . . bringing her to a mind-shattering orgasm.

She became intensely aware of Shane's muscular body close to hers . . . and of the fact she was all alone with him, in a quiet corridor where no one would see them. A fiery need blazed through her.

"I don't really want to go into the details. . . ."

"But—"

"Shane, I . . ."

How could she tell him what she wanted? She wanted to feel his arms around her . . . to feel his solid masculine chest pressed against her . . . to feel his lips on her . . . her mouth . . . her breasts . . . God, on her raging clit.

"What is it, Summer?" Shane's warm blue eyes peered into hers.

"I've wanted you for a long time."

Shane stared at Summer, gazing at him with intense longing in her sapphire blue eyes. His heart pumped loudly. She wanted him? Good God, he had to hold himself back from sliding his arms around her and plundering her lips. But he was afraid that once he got his hands on her, he wouldn't want to stop at a kiss. Once he felt the softness of her body pressed against him, like an addiction, he would want more and more. He would likely pull her into the nearest room and ravage her.

Thoughts of some guy touching her body, ordering her to do things . . . Possessiveness washed through him. *He* wanted Summer.

Her hands slid to his cheeks and she moved closer. He breathed in the delicate fragrance of spring blossoms emanating from her lovely auburn hair. Her eyes glittered as her face drew nearer. She was going to kiss him. Damn, he had dreamed of this forever.

He met her lips gently, holding back the force of his passion, not wanting to scare her, but the sound of her small gasp jolted him. His arms wrapped around her, and he tugged her against his body. His cock rose at the feel of her . . . at the knowledge she was turned on . . . by him.

She wrapped her arms around his neck and clung to him. Her lips moved frantically on his. Her soft breasts pressed into his chest, and her pebble-hard nipples tormented him. He wanted to slide his hands under her soft sweater and stroke her naked breasts . . . cup her hard nipples in the palm of his hand.

He clung to her, holding her tight against him, gliding his tongue along hers . . . and so totally turned on that he was afraid he was going to lose it right then and there.

Her lips slipped from his, and she nuzzled his neck.

"Oh, Shane . . ."

She glanced up at him. Her cheeks were stained crimson.

"I'm . . . uh . . ." She sucked in a deep breath.

"It's okay, sweetheart. I—"

The sound of someone clearing his throat stopped him dead.

Summer sighed. Oh, God, it was bad enough she'd thrown herself at Shane in the middle of the corridor . . . now someone had *seen* them.

"Don't you think this is a little inappropriate?" said Kyle.

Eight

As soon as Kyle had seen Summer in Shane's arms, his gut had clenched and his hands tightened into fists. At the same time, his cock had swelled at her murmured sounds of pleasure.

How had he missed the signs? Summer and his best friend were involved. How long had it been going on? Why had they hidden it from him?

Feelings of betrayal spiked through him.

"Summer. In my office. Now."

She moved away from Shane and stepped down the corridor without looking in Kyle's direction.

"Kyle, it's not what you think," Shane said.

He glared at Shane, not dignifying his comment with an answer.

Shane followed Summer, catching up to her in a few long strides, clearly intending to accompany her to Kyle's office.

"Shane, you're needed at the front desk," Kyle said in a tight voice. "A security issue."

Shane's jaw twitched. Clearly he was torn between his professional responsibility and staying by Summer's side.

Summer rested her hand on Shane's arm. Kyle gritted his teeth at the sight.

"It's okay. Go," Summer said.

Shane nodded, then reluctantly stepped past Summer and strode down the hall toward the lobby.

Summer started walking again, Kyle following behind her. She turned down the corridor on the left before the lobby, glad she didn't have to parade across the lobby—not with her face blazing with heat.

She walked past his secretary's desk, which was vacant at the moment, and into Kyle's office.

She could feel his ominous presence behind her. She'd never felt like his employee before. In fact, she wasn't his employee, but he could end the contract for her to sell chocolates in the hotel at any time—which would be a disaster. She got wonderful traffic here at an affordable rent. When the tour buses came brimming with tourists from May to October, her sales went through the roof.

But her worries about her business and whether she'd continue to have a viable livelihood were not her main concern. She didn't really think Kyle would toss her out. What made her heart ache was that she might have hurt him.

The door closed, and she could feel him move closer. Slowly, she turned around. At the sight of the anxiety in his eyes, her heart compressed.

"Kyle, I'm so sorry, I—"

With a quick movement, he tugged her toward him and captured her mouth with his. She barely had time to catch her breath when his tongue swept across her lips . . . and she opened for him. He stroked inside with a sweet caress, and she melted against him. His arms encircled her and held her close to his body. Her breasts pressed hard against his muscular chest and . . . she felt a bulge against her stomach.

He was hard. He wanted her.

Or was that just because he'd witnessed her in another man's arms?

His lips parted from hers, and he stared at her with hunger in his eyes.

"Summer, I want you. I have for a long time."

Kyle wanted her. Joy washed through her at the thought. She wanted him. He wanted her.

But what about Shane? Was he attracted to her, too? Sure, he'd kissed her, but she had taken the lead. He hadn't said anything to indicate his feelings for her.

Kyle released her and stepped back, giving her space to breathe.

"I just wanted you to know that."

He sat on one of the chairs by the circular table, rather than behind his desk, and gestured for her to take the chair next to him.

"How long have you and Shane been . . . involved romantically?"

"We're not. That was . . ." She waved her hand vaguely. "It just happened."

"It was a pretty spectacular happening."

Her cheeks flushed. "I know. It was . . . strange. I'm just . . . in a weird mood these days."

"You met someone when you were away."

It wasn't a question.

She sighed. "Yes."

"You . . . slept with him?"

She nodded.

"So this . . . fling . . . it's the reason you're in this 'weird mood.' In other words, you're not willing to go back to having essentially no sex life."

She just stared at him, her mouth dropping open.

"I . . . uh . . . guess that's true."

She didn't like the fact he thought she had no love life. It was true, but she didn't like him knowing it.

He sat back in his chair and grabbed a pen from the tabletop. He flipped it over and over as he studied her face.

"You and I and Shane . . . we've all been avoiding what has become more and more obvious. Shane and I are both attracted to you . . . and I think that you are attracted to both of us." He raised an eyebrow, but she made no move to acknowledge his theory. She had no idea if Kyle was guessing at Shane's attraction to her or if he'd actually spoken to Shane about it. She doubted the latter.

Kyle leaned forward.

"We've all been avoiding doing anything about the situation because of our friendship . . . worried about changing the status quo for fear of someone getting hurt."

Her lips tightened into a straight line.

He dropped the pen onto the table.

"I think it's about time the three of us had a little talk."

When Summer arrived at Kyle's house on Friday evening—for the "little talk"—Shane was already there. He opened the door when she knocked and led her into the living room.

She knew Kyle was attracted to her—he had told her so in his office—but what about Shane? Maybe he was here just to let her down easy and give his blessing for her to date Kyle.

That certainly would make the whole situation easier.

Except for her continued attraction to him. Even now, the tangy scent of his aftershave sent memories of that sensational kiss swirling through her . . . of his hard, masculine body pressed against hers . . .

He drew her close, her breasts pressed against his muscular chest, and he kissed her with a subdued passion. Her pulse began to accelerate. He drew back and gazed at her, his blue eyes dazzling in their intensity.

"I know Kyle told you how he feels about you. I just want you to know I'm crazy about you, too."

"You two at it again?" Kyle grinned from the kitchen doorway, then he strode toward her.

He drew her from Shane and wrapped his strong arms around her. His sea green eyes boiled with passion as he captured her mouth in a heart-stopping kiss, his lips moving sensuously on hers, leaving her breathless.

When he released her, Summer slumped down on the couch. "So I'm attracted to both of you, and you're both attracted to me." She sighed. "This is a real mess."

The memory of Max's words—*Why not go out with both . . . a threesome . . . then you don't have to choose*—skittered through her head. Ever since he'd said it, the idea had haunted her . . . filled her dreams.

A ménage à trois.

"We'll figure something out," Kyle said. "For now, let's relax and have some dinner. I've got some steaks here, and I've started the barbecue. Let's go outside and enjoy the evening, then we'll discuss things."

Shane and Summer followed Kyle into the kitchen.

"Want some sangria?"

"Sure." Summer watched Kyle pour some from a full pitcher. The ice in the glass cracked loudly.

She took the glass and sipped, enjoying the cold, fruity wine. Kyle grabbed the platter of steaks, and Shane took the large salad bowl. Summer picked up the pitcher and followed them into the backyard.

Kyle opened the barbecue lid and set the steaks on the grill. Summer sat on one of the deck chairs and glanced over at the gorgeous kidney-shaped pool. The sky was alight with orange-and-purple clouds as the sun set, invisible behind the trees across the back of Kyle's large yard. His house backed onto a ravine, and a tall hedge along each side of his yard, along with the fact that there was quite a distance between his yard and those of his two side neighbors, allowed him a great deal of privacy.

It was great living in a small town where there was space to have such large yards.

The aroma of steaks grilling quickly filled the air.

"Kyle, is your dad coming to visit for the July long weekend?" Summer asked. Kyle's birthday was at the end of July, and his dad's summer visits doubled as a birthday visit.

"No, he can't make it this year. And as usual, he can't tell me why because everything's always critical in the military, especially at his level."

Summer understood the irritation in Kyle's voice. He resented the military. Blamed it for the distance—both emotional and physical—between him and his dad.

Kyle loved his father, but he had spent too many years moving around as a child, leaving friends behind, having to learn how to fit into a new school . . . a new town . . .

Until he'd met Shane. When Kyle's family had moved

here, the friendship he'd formed with Shane lasted, even after they moved away again. They decided to go to the same college, then Kyle moved here for good . . . and never looked back.

"You mean I don't get to hear the admiral's views on my quitting the force at our annual barbecue?" asked Shane, eyebrows raised. "Damn, that's the highlight of my year."

"Sorry, buddy," Kyle responded. "*I* can nag you a bit, if you want."

Shane sighed as if in disappointment. "Naw. It's just not the same."

Kyle chuckled. Kyle's dad and Shane got on amazingly well, probably because Shane understood the older man's views and realized he made the comments he did only because he liked Shane and truly wanted to help.

Summer watched as Kyle flipped the steaks, Shane leaning against the deck railing, giving advice about how to tell if they were done well enough. Although these two men had very different personalities—Shane never took anything too seriously and Kyle was more the strong, silent type—they were as close as two friends could be. They would do anything for each other.

Even share a woman?

Kyle piled the steaks onto a plate and set them on the table. Soon all three of them enjoyed the meal while watching the sun set. Summer took a bite of the tender meat and chewed thoughtfully. After dinner, they would discuss what to do about the fact that both men were attracted to her.

What would Kyle and Shane suggest? Would they make her pick one of them? She didn't want to do that.

She could date both of them, but then it would be . . . different between them. And awkward when they were all together.

Would it really make sense to go for a ménage à trois? To date . . . and have sex . . . with both of them at the same time?

Excitement quivered through her at the thought of being with both of them. Shane and Kyle both touching her at the same time . . . she touching both of them. One cock in each of her hands. Wrapping her lips around one big, hard cock while the other man stroked her breasts.

Heat surged through her. She grasped her icy glass and sipped the sangria.

Would Shane and Kyle go for such a thing?

She glanced at Kyle as he returned to the deck after carrying the empty dinner plates inside. His shirt was open, showing off his hard, sculpted abs. She glanced at Shane, who put the cover over the barbecue, then sat down across from her and sent her a dazzling smile. Her gaze fell to his lips, and she remembered the kiss in the corridor . . . how it had sent her blood sizzling.

Oh, God, she hoped so.

But she would have to suggest it, because she was sure *they* wouldn't.

She glanced from one to the other. But how?

She stretched out her legs and watched the solar lights come on around the pool—set to turn on automatically when it got dark. Small ripples across the water glittered in the soft twilight.

Maybe a little subtle persuasion. If she showed them what she wanted . . .

Kyle watched Summer sitting deep in thought and wondered what was going through her head.

"It's a warm night," Summer said. "It would be nice to go for a swim."

She began to unfasten the buttons of her blouse.

"You brought your bathing suit?" Kyle asked.

Her gaze locked with his. "No . . . I didn't."

He couldn't tell exactly what was going on behind those sapphire blue eyes.

As she released the last button, he realized she was wearing a lacy pink bra beneath her shirt, not one of her bright-colored bikinis. As she slipped off her top, revealing the pink lace-and-satin garment, his heart beat faster. Even though he'd seen her in some pretty skimpy bikinis, it wasn't the same as actually seeing her in a bra. She could wear a bathing suit on the most crowded of beaches and it would be totally acceptable, but seeing her in her lacy undergarment was . . . intimate.

Except that Shane was here, too.

His heart pumped faster. What exactly did Summer have in mind?

She let the blouse slide from her arms, then she scooped up the garment and tossed it into her large bag. She sat still for a few moments, glancing over the backyard . . . not at him or Shane . . . seeming a little ill at ease.

Well, she couldn't be as ill at ease as either him—he adjusted his jeans over his growing cock—or Shane. His friend sent him a questioning glance, then returned his gaze to Summer . . . and the soft, round curve of her lace-covered breasts. Her erect nipples showed clearly through the satiny fabric below the lace edges.

She brushed her hair behind her ear and shifted in her chair. She seemed uncomfortable, but damn it, what was he supposed to do about it? She'd started this.

"Uh . . . Summer, don't get me wrong, I love the view, but . . . What's going on?" Shane asked.

She gazed at him, seeming lost in thought. "I'm . . . uh . . . just hot, that's all."

Holy hell, she wasn't kidding about that. She was extremely hot. And she was making *him* hot. Shane, too, from the look of his growing bulge.

Did Summer want them to do something? To move things forward? If so, she'd put them in an extremely difficult situation.

Summer gripped the arms of the chair. Why had she started this? She felt way out of her depth. Of course, she found it wildly exciting that she might wind up having sex with both Shane and Kyle . . . at the same time.

A threesome.

The thought of both their hands touching her . . . stroking her . . . sent tingles through her body.

She sucked in a breath. She had taken the first step. No sense stopping now. She tucked her hands behind her and released the hooks of her bra, then slid the straps off her shoulders. Not daring to glance at either man on the deck, she eased the bra forward and slid it off. The warm breeze brushed across her skin, and her nipples puckered even tighter.

Now both Shane and Kyle stared at her openly, not even

pretending not to notice her rigid nipples as they thrust forward. She could feel their hot gazes like a soft caress.

Oh, God, it was so sinfully erotic sitting here with her breasts naked, these two hot guys, who had both told her they wanted her, looking at her so intently.

She brushed her hands over her breasts. The nipples stroked along her palms. She slid her fingertips over the hard buds. That and the hungry look in Shane's and Kyle's eyes sent blazing heat through her.

She slid her hands under her breasts and lifted them as though offering them to the men.

"Do you . . ." She stroked her breasts again, feeling the thrum in her body. "Do you want me?"

"Of course we want you, Summer," Shane said, but instead of rushing toward her and dragging her into his arms, he glanced hesitantly toward Kyle.

Just tell them you want them to fuck you. Both of them.

That's what Tanya would tell her to do. But . . . she couldn't say that. Not to Kyle and Shane.

Kyle stood up and stepped toward her, then took her hand and drew her to her feet.

"Sweetheart, we do want you. I want to touch those glorious breasts of yours. I want to make love to you." He leaned toward her and murmured in her ear, "Do you want both Shane and me to make love to you? Is that it?"

That's what Summer wanted all right, but . . . When she gazed into Kyle's simmering emerald eyes . . . and realized he might actually go for it . . . that in a few minutes, both men might be touching her breasts, freeing their cocks to her, she sucked in a breath.

Oh, God, what had she been thinking? She couldn't do something so outrageous as having a ménage à trois. Not here in Port Smith. Not with her friends . . . no matter how much she wanted them to be *more* than friends.

She couldn't do this.

As soon as Kyle saw the uncertainty in Summer's sapphire eyes . . . the vulnerability . . . he knew he had played this wrong.

"I . . ." She shook her head and backed away from him. She snatched up her bag and dodged into the house. He could see her tugging on her blouse as she dashed across the living room, then out the front door to her car.

"Should we go after her?" Shane asked.

"No. I think that would freak her out even more."

Kyle picked up the pink bra still lying on the table, quite aware that only moments before, these lacy cups had been wrapped around Summer's delightful breasts.

"She needs a little time. She's clearly embarrassed by what she did tonight. We have to be really careful to put her at ease the next time we see her."

Summer closed the door behind her and leaned against it, trying to catch her breath. She'd driven home braless with her blouse buttoned crookedly, praying she wouldn't be pulled over. She'd just wanted to get home . . . and away from Shane and Kyle.

She felt like such a fool.

And the whole situation had left her brimming with sexual need.

Summer noticed the light flashing on her answering

machine. Was the message from Shane or Kyle? She pressed the button and heard Max's voice asking her to call him when she got in and giving her his cell number.

She picked up the phone and dialed. He answered after two rings.

"Hi, Max. It's Summer."

"Are you okay? You sound a little down."

She sucked in a breath and calmed her voice. "I'm fine."

It wasn't true. Her pulse was racing, her heart pounding in her chest . . . and she felt sick.

"Okay. Do you mind if I get back to you in about twenty minutes?" Max asked.

"Sure. No problem. I'll be here."

After she hung up, she grabbed herself a tall glass of water and headed for the living room, intending to forget her troubles by watching a little TV. She turned on the set and flipped around the channels until she found an old movie, then settled back on the couch. She fidgeted as she watched, but it didn't really keep her attention, and before long she found herself staring at the clock, wondering when Max would call back. A knock sounded at the door and she stood up to answer it.

What if it was Kyle or Shane? Or both?

She peered through the sidelight and . . .

Max!

Nine

Summer tugged open the door, a broad smile stretching her face. Max stood on her doorstep, his face even more devastatingly handsome than she remembered. She wanted to run her fingers through his black, spiky hair, to glide them down the well-defined muscles of his bare chest. To basically tear off his clothes and kiss every hard, masculine part of him. Then ravage him thoroughly and completely.

"What are you doing here?" She clung to the edge of the door, drinking in the sight of him. She couldn't believe he'd come all the way from New York to see her.

"I thought I'd surprise you. Tanya gave me your address. She thought you'd be okay with a weekend guest." He raised his eyebrows expectantly.

What the heck was she thinking, making him wait on the doorstep? She loosened her grip on the door and stepped back.

"Come in."

He had neatly invited himself to stay at her house . . . and she was thrilled. She stepped into his strong arms and breathed in his spicy male scent as he held her close, his broad chest solid against her breasts. He captured her lips in a long, passionate kiss. Finally, he eased away and grabbed his bag from the porch, then placed it inside.

"I'm glad you're here," she said.

He slid his arm around her waist and walked toward the couch, then sat beside her.

"Okay. Now, tell me what's wrong."

She crumpled against him and told him the whole story about what had happened at Kyle's. He held her, his strong presence soothing her.

"I wanted to make it all work . . . ," she said. "I thought showing them what I wanted . . . But I just couldn't do it."

"It's okay, sweetheart," he said, his voice warm and understanding.

"Now they probably think I'm a . . . a . . ." She sighed. "I don't know what, but something really embarrassing."

He smiled as he stroked her hair behind her ear. "I'm sure they don't. From what you've told me, they really care about you. They aren't going to think anything bad about you."

She gazed up at him and searched his eyes. She had known Max only as the strong Dominant, but now she saw another side of him. Warm and compassionate.

As soon as Max had seen Summer at the door, he'd known something was wrong. As she told him her story, he could feel the embarrassment and conflict in her words. At the same time, he couldn't help imagining her stripping off her top and bra . . . exposing her naked breasts. How had those guys resisted jumping at the opportunity she'd offered them?

Now her sapphire blue eyes stared up at him with quiet

vulnerability, and she leaned forward and brushed her lips on his with a sweet tenderness he found almost unnerving.

Damn, somehow this woman affected him in a way no other had in a very long time.

He leaned back, needing a little distance right now. Then he saw that her collar wasn't sitting right. The buttons were done up in the wrong holes.

"I notice your blouse is in disarray," he observed, grinning.

Her hand fluttered to her chest. "I left in a hurry."

Summer unfastened the middle buttons, intending to refasten them in the appropriate holes, but the heat of Max's gaze ignited the frustrated arousal bubbling through her from earlier. She was intensely aware of his hot male gaze on her fingers as she released first one button, then another. Instead of refastening them, she continued to unfasten the ones below, then the ones above.

Slowly, she parted her blouse, exposing her naked breasts to him. His smoky gray eyes darkened to charcoal.

"You are looking very sexy tonight."

She ran her fingers over her nipples. The hard buds jutted forward as though reaching for Max. She twirled her finger around one nipple, then the other. Hot tremors rippled through her.

"I have something for you." He stood up and grabbed his bag. "I'll show it to you . . . in the bedroom."

She smiled and stood up, then led him to her room. He reached inside his bag and pulled out a long box, then handed it to her. It was a vibrator that looked like a big, blue cock.

"It's like the little egg vibrator, in that I can control it from a distance." He set his bag beside the chair facing the end of her bed, then sat down.

"Open the package." The note of authority in his voice sent a thrill through her.

"Yes, Master," she responded automatically. She opened the box, then pulled out the big cock. It felt quite substantial in her hand.

"Give me the remote, then put the cock beside the bed."

She placed it on the bedside table, anticipation quivering through her, knowing he intended to use the toy and she would pretend he was making love to her. She would pretend his long, hard cock was inside her, pumping into her, making her come. And she really wanted to come. Hard and long.

"Give me the remote."

She pulled the small remote out of the box and walked toward Max, placed it in his outstretched hand, then dropped the empty box on her dresser.

With that remote, he would control when and how she came. The thought sent a shiver of excitement through her.

"Now go to the bed and take off your pants."

She strolled toward the bed with a swing to her hips, then, with her back to Max, unfastened her jeans and pushed them to the floor. While still bent over, she pivoted her hips, to give him a great view of her ass in the pink lace thong, then she stood up and glanced over her shoulder. Slowly, she turned around. She stood there and smiled in anticipation, awaiting his command.

"Summer, remove that incredibly sexy thong."

She hooked her fingers under the elastic and rolled the

garment down her legs, then kicked it toward him. It caught on the chair and hung jauntily from the armrest.

"Prop up the pillows and lie down on the bed."

A quiver stole through her as she plumped up two of her four pillows and stacked them at an angle, then climbed onto the bed.

"Open your legs. Let me see your pretty pussy."

She drew in a deep breath and spread her knees wide. Cool air washed across moist, intimate folds, which only made her hotter.

"Lovely. Now stroke your pussy."

She ran her fingers along her slit.

"Tell me what it feels like."

"It's very wet." Her fingers glided through the slickness.

"What else?"

"And hot. Wet and hot."

"What would you like right now?"

She smiled. "I would like your long, hard cock inside my wet pussy . . . Master."

Oh, God, it felt so sexy to talk dirty like this.

"Wouldn't you like to touch my cock first?"

"Yes, I'd like to wrap my hand around it and pump it up and down. Then I'd kneel down in front of you and kiss it. Lick the end."

"Yes?"

The thought of his long, hot cock in her hands sent her blood boiling.

"Then I'd take it in my mouth and I'd suck it." She could just imagine her lips surrounding him, his hardness solid within her mouth.

"Oh, yes."

He unzipped his pants and pulled out his cock. It was fully erect . . . and looked absolutely delicious. She longed to suck on that thick, hard cock head right now.

"I'd love to feel your mouth on my cock. But I have another idea." He reached into his bag and pulled out a cellophane package. He crossed the room and handed it to her. "A lovely woman gave this to me at the Sex-à-la-Gala show, and I think right now is the perfect time to use it."

It was the flesh-colored chocolate cock she'd given him. Max sat back in the chair.

"Pretend that's me and show me what you'd do."

She smiled and unwrapped the cock, then held it in her hand. It was so realistic looking, though nowhere near as big as Max's. She licked the tip, then circled her tongue around the ridge under the head.

"Oh, sweetheart." He squeezed his cock mercilessly.

She licked the shaft, then took the tip in her mouth. The taste of sweet chocolate filled her mouth. The chocolate penis was hard and broad, but not hot like Max. She longed to feel his kid leather skin under her tongue, feel his steel hardness within her mouth.

She drew the cock into her mouth, then out. She licked the tip, then sucked it in again, the whole time locking her gaze with Max's. His hand moved up and down on the cock she wanted with such hunger. She thrust the sweet cock in and out of her mouth, then pulled it deep and sucked.

"Summer, are you sucking on it?"

She nodded. His simmering charcoal eyes watched her, intense with longing. He wanted her.

"Pick up the blue cock," he said.

She drew the candy cock from her mouth and laid it on

the table, then picked up the toy cock and stroked it over her chest.

"Lay it down between your breasts."

Her vagina ached for him. She wanted to stuff the cock inside to relieve this devilish yearning. But she obeyed him, wanting him to command her.

"Summer, do you have another dildo?"

"Of course, Master."

"Get it."

She grabbed the cock lying between her breasts, then leaned sideways to reach the drawer on the bedside table. She reached inside and pulled out her usual vibrator, which was long and slim with a suction cup base.

"Now lay it down beside you, lie back, and close your eyes."

She placed the two cocks beside her, relaxed against the pillows, and closed her eyes.

"Relax and pretend you're lying all alone in your room. Imagine it's late at night and you're lonely and wildly turned on."

No imagining needed there.

"A door opens and someone comes into the room."

She imagined she heard footsteps, then her bedroom door open.

"This someone approaches the bed."

Imagined footsteps approached across the hardwood floor.

"He's standing right beside it. Don't open your eyes. Just wait. He's looking at you. At your sexy, naked body."

She had to stop her hands from covering herself. It felt so real.

"It's Shane. Watching you. Wanting you."

She imagined Shane standing over her. She could feel the heat of his gaze.

"The sound of a door opening . . . your bedroom door again . . ."

Her eyelids flickered, but she managed to keep them closed.

"Now Kyle is here, too. The door closes. You can hear him approach the bed."

She sucked in a breath, imagining both Kyle and Shane standing over her. Looking at her.

"They both sit on the bed beside you, one on each side. Kyle strokes your breast."

Her breath held. She wanted so badly to feel Kyle's hands on her.

"Stroke your breast, Summer. Pretend Kyle is doing it."

She stroked her hand over her right breast, then cupped it. The nipple jutted into her palm.

"Now Shane is stroking your other breast."

She brought her other hand to that breast and stroked lightly, as she imagined Shane would do, then she pinched the nipple.

"Good. They're both stroking and teasing your nipples."

She tweaked and teased her hard nubs. She licked her index finger and thumb and surrounded one tight nipple. She pretended Shane's mouth enveloped her hard, distended flesh.

"They both want you, Summer. They both want to fuck you."

She moaned as both hands caressed and cajoled her breasts.

"Pick up the dildo and slide it into your pussy."

Groping for the two cocks lying beside her, she found the flat suction cup base easily without opening her eyes, not wanting to lose the intense image of both Shane and Kyle stroking her.

She pressed it against her wet slit and slid it inside.

"That's Kyle sliding inside you. Just once, all the way in, then he slides out."

She slid it deeper, then pulled it out, moaning at the loss.

"Grab the extra pillows beside you and tuck them under your hips, lifting that glorious ass in the air. Let Kyle and Shane see that beautiful pussy of yours."

She reached for her spare pillows and followed his orders.

"Now imagine Kyle is lying beneath you and he presses the tip of his cock to your anus and slowly pushes inside."

She pushed the slick cock against her back opening and eased it inside. Slowly . . . pushing with her internal muscles to allow the cock to slide inside. Then those muscles grabbed it and pulled it inside, until the base pressed against her ass, stopping it from disappearing inside.

"Kyle groans at the way your ass grips him so tightly."

She groaned at the way he filled her so full.

"Now pick up your new cock."

She grabbed it, anticipation strumming through her.

"Shane climbs over you and kisses you passionately."

She could imagine his mouth taking hers, while Kyle's arms held her around the waist, his cock fully embedded in her ass.

"Shane's cock presses against your slit, then slides into you."

She slid her fingers along her slit and into her opening, then pressed the cock to it. She eased it inside. It was Shane's cock. Gliding inside her at last. And Kyle's cock, filling her from behind.

Both of them. Oh, God. She quivered as Shane's cock filled her deeply.

Now it was fully immersed in her. She lay there, breathing deeply, enjoying the intense fullness of Kyle and Shane inside her.

Shane's cock, deep inside her vagina, started to vibrate. She gasped. Then it began to move, spiraling in a circle. The little fingerlike device on the base rippled against her clit.

"Oh, yes!" she roared. She sucked in air and squirmed, her hand planted firmly over the base of Shane's cock so it wouldn't slip out.

Reality seemed to swirl and wash away as intense pleasure filled her. Her clit quivered and she squeezed her legs tight, squeezing Shane's cock inside her and Kyle's cock tight inside her ass.

"They're making you come, Summer," Max said. "Let me see you come."

Intense pleasure washed over her, and she wailed as it swept her away.

"Are you coming, Summer?"

"Yes." She exhaled sharply. "They're making me come. I'm . . . ahhh . . ." She sucked in air at the blissful rush. "Coming!" As the pleasure flushed through her, she added quickly, "Master."

It wasn't just the thought of Kyle and Shane fucking her that had made her come. It had been Max and his direction. His remote vibrator.

His voice of authority.

He had brought her fantasy to life, and he'd ridden right along with her. Her master of pleasure.

"Open your eyes, Summer."

She opened her eyes and smiled. Max was still fully erect, his cock still in his grasp.

"Your cock is so big and hard, Master." She licked her lips and stared at it. "Wouldn't you like me to lick it, then suck it into my mouth?"

"Oh, yes, I'd like that." He grinned. "But right now you're lying on your bed with two men's cocks inside you."

She grinned. "Then would you like Shane to slide out and make room for you?"

"Yes." His fiery gaze linked with hers.

She pulled the cock out of her vagina and laid it beside her. She widened her legs to give him a better view of her wet opening.

He stood up with coal-hot eyes and dropped his pants to the floor, then strode to the bed.

"I'm going to slide my hard cock into you."

"Oh, yes, Master. Please."

He prowled over her and pressed his cock head to her opening, then thrust inside. She gasped.

"Oh, Master. It feels so good."

Having his hot, real-life cock glide into her sent incredible sensations rushing through her, intensified by the cock still in her ass.

"Your cock inside me feels so . . ."

He thrust again. She moaned, throwing her head back.

"Your cock is so big. It's driving so deep."

"Oh, sweetheart," Max groaned. "I'm going to . . ."

He pumped harder.

"You're making me come, Master. Oh, yes. Oh . . . ," she wailed, in the grip of an intense orgasm.

Hot liquid filled her as she clung to Max's broad shoulders.

"Ohhhh, Master." She gasped and fell back against the pillows, the cock in her ass a reminder of the wild, intense fantasy they'd played out before their lovemaking.

Kyle and Shane.

And Max.

She fell asleep with the cock in her ass. She had at least one orgasm in the depths of the night, during dreams of her three special men taking turns filling her from every angle.

On Monday morning, Summer sat at the desk in her office off the back of the store and sighed. Max had left last night, and she already missed him. They'd made love all weekend—he just couldn't seem to get enough of her—and she realized she wanted a lot more of him.

But he was gone, and she had to move forward. One thing for sure, she didn't want to go back to a nonexistent sex life.

She stared at the inventory displayed on her computer screen while rolling her metallic blue pen between her fingers. The pictures of gift boxes, varied sizes of cellophane bags, and gold and silver twist ties could not hold her attention. It drifted back to Friday night. To Max's voice painting a vivid image in her mind of Kyle beneath her . . . of Shane on top. Of their two hard cocks inside her.

She shifted on her chair, her intimate muscles squeezing

on nothing as she longed for just one of those cocks right now.

Shane. Or Kyle. Before the Sex-à-la-Gala show, she'd kept her feelings for both of them locked inside, unwilling to risk their friendship. Now, she'd kissed Shane, stripped in front of both of them . . . and if either one of them was to walk into this office right now—

"There you are."

She dropped the pen and spun around at the sound of Shane's voice.

Shane watched her glossy auburn hair swirl around her face as she turned to face him, her sapphire eyes wide.

"Sorry, Summer, I didn't mean to startle you, but there was no one in the store and nobody came out when the bell over the door sounded." He raised an eyebrow. "You could lose a lot of inventory that way."

Not that the type of people who stayed at the hotel tended to steal, but she should still be careful.

"Oh, right. I heard the bell, but I forgot Cindy went to Accounting to get some change."

That wasn't like Summer.

Her gaze trailed from his face, down his chest, then unnervingly came to rest on his crotch before diverting back to his face. His groin ached at the realization that she was checking him out. An image from Friday night stormed through him—Summer sliding her blouse from her shoulders, revealing her lacy pink bra . . . then divesting herself of the bra . . . her fingers stroking over her hard nipples . . . His cock swelled, straining against his jeans.

Damn, he'd better say what he came here to say before he was too far gone.

"Summer, about the other night. Is everything okay?"

Her gaze darted to his. "What do you mean?"

He didn't want to mention her undressing.

"The way you left. I . . . just wanted to make sure everything is okay between us . . . all of us."

Summer remembered the feel of the breeze on her naked breasts. Her fingertips stroking over her nipples while Shane and Kyle stared at her with heated expressions.

"You seemed a little embarrassed," Shane said, "and I wanted to assure you, there's no problem as far as I'm concerned. We can totally forget the incident if that's what you want."

Her breasts ached. But she couldn't forget the incident. And she couldn't forget the hungry look in his eyes as he'd watched her cup and lift her breasts to him.

The hunger returned to his eyes as she stared at him. She licked her dry lips. Friday night had awakened a need so overwhelming, she didn't think she could hide it anymore. She wanted Shane . . . and Kyle.

But Shane was here right now. Big and masculine . . . his gaze burning through her.

She stood up and stepped toward him. "Do you want to forget it?"

"I . . . uh . . . I'm just not sure what you want."

She pressed her hand to his broad, flat chest. Solid muscle. *Right now, I want you.*

But she didn't say it. She stroked her hand over his chest, then down to his tightly sculpted stomach. She could feel the ripple of muscle through his thin cotton shirt. He stood stiff, clearly unsure what to do. He slid one arm around her waist as she tilted her head and nuzzled her lips against the crook of his neck. The scent of a tangy ocean breeze filled her nostrils, and she licked his salty skin. His pulse raced beneath her tongue.

Her nipples hardened against him, and she could feel wetness pooling between her legs. Oh, God, she wanted him so badly.

Shane was here. Now.

Her hand stroked downward . . . and caught on his pager. Security. Shane was trained as a police officer. He'd carried a gun at one time and . . .

She stroked her index finger down his chest.

"Shane, do you have . . . handcuffs?"

Ten

Summer felt Shane's arm clamp tight around her.

The thought of him snapping the metal bracelets around her wrists . . . leaving her helpless to his roving hands . . . sent heat storming through her.

"Uh . . . not *with* me."

Summer grasped Shane's handsome face with both hands, then pushed herself up on tiptoes and captured his lips with hers. His arms slid around her and he clutched her to him, his mouth moving passionately on hers. Her breasts crushed against his hard chest. She found it hard to breathe. His tongue spiked into her mouth, and she opened, then sucked deeper.

With mouths still locked, she spun them around and eased Shane back against the desk. Her hands found the zipper at his swelling crotch and pulled the tag down. Her fingers slipped inside and she stroked over rock-hard flesh straining to be free of the thin cotton fabric. She found the opening and slid inside.

Hot. Silky. Hard.

She wrapped her hand around his cock and drew it out.

"Honey, we—" Shane's hoarse voice caught, and he cleared his throat. "We shouldn't be doing this here."

She glanced toward the door. Shane had closed it when he'd come in.

"The door is closed. Cindy won't disturb us."

She stroked his hard cock again. "Shane, I want you."

She took his hand and rested it on her breast. Instantly, he cupped his hand and stroked. She released his wonderful cock, grabbed the hem of her blouse, and, ignoring the buttons, pulled it over her head. Shane's cobalt blue gaze locked on her chest as she reached behind her and flicked open the hooks of her crimson bra. She dropped it to the floor. His gaze seared her as it lingered on her puckering nipples.

"You are so beautiful."

She grasped his big hand and placed it over one naked, aching breast.

"Do you want me, Shane?"

Her hand found his rigid cock again, straining straight out of his fly. She wrapped her fingers around it and stroked.

"Oh, God, yes."

She kissed him again, reveling in the feel of his mouth on hers. She had yearned for this for so long. Shane was sweet and protective and caring. She loved being with him, and she knew that, given time, the feelings of friendship and affection between them would turn to love. A deep and lasting love.

He leaned down and drew one of her nipples into his mouth. She moaned at the exquisite feel of his moist tongue lapping against her, then of being drawn deep into the heat of his mouth.

Foreplay was a wonderful thing, but she needed that big cock of his inside her.

She shimmied out of her panties, then drew her skirt upward. Shane wrapped his hands around her waist and lifted her to the desk, then stepped between her thighs.

"Is this what you want, sweetheart?"

He pressed the tip of his big cock against her slick opening.

"Oh, yes. . . ." She clung to his shoulders as he stroked her with his cock head, his powerful, hard flesh moving up and down her slit. Then he pushed forward a fraction of an inch, poised and ready to thrust inside her. She whimpered, wanting him so bad she couldn't think straight.

She curled her fingers around his ear and nuzzled his cheek. He kissed her, passion and lust flaring like sparks off a welding torch. His cock head burned against her sensitive flesh. He pushed his cock a tiny bit forward, then drew back, and she moaned. He pressed forward a little again, only half his cock head sliding into her before he eased back.

"Oh, God, fuck me, Shane."

He thrust forward, and his long shaft filled her. She gasped at the exhilarating invasion. He held her tight to his body. Neither of them moved for a heartbeat, then he drew back.

"You are so hot, honey. God, I've waited so long to do this."

She smiled. "So why wait any longer? I'm not fragile, you know."

He grinned, then thrust deep into her. She gasped again as his hard length filled her. He drew back and thrust, drew back and thrust. The incredible pleasure built in a steady rhythm, washing through her, expanding to encompass her entire awareness.

His hands cupped her buttocks and he pulled her tighter

to his body, driving his cock deeper still. An explosion flared inside her, and she moaned as pleasure soared through her, expanding in tumultuous waves of bliss.

She cried out, and Shane drove deep, then pulsed inside her.

They clung to each other as their breathing returned to normal. He gazed down at her, a sweet softness in his blue eyes.

"Summer, I've wanted you for so long. I can't believe—"

"We finally did it in my office?" she quipped.

He grinned. "Well, yeah, that's been a hot fantasy of mine for a while, but I mean . . ." His grin faded, and he stroked a random strand of hair from her face. "What do we do about Kyle?"

Her heart clenched. Oh, damn, of course Shane would believe this meant she'd chosen him over Kyle.

She stroked his cheek. "Shane, I want you. You obviously know that. But I want Kyle, too. Is there any way we could find a way to . . . share?"

"You want to have an intimate relationship with both Kyle and me?"

She nodded.

"So you'd alternate dates with us? Having sex with both of us?"

"Not exactly."

This was even harder than she'd thought. How could she tell him she wanted to have sex with both of them at the same time?

"You don't want to date both of us?" His brow furrowed in confusion.

Her cell phone rang, but she'd be damned if she'd answer

it with Shane still fully immersed in her, the afterglow of their intimacy still clinging to them. Shane glanced at her purse.

"Whoever it is will call back." She wrapped her arms around Shane's neck. "Right now you feel so good inside me. Let's talk about what we'll do about Kyle later."

She squeezed his cock with her intimate muscles, and his semierect member hardened. She stroked her naked breast, then teased the nipple to a hard nub. His gaze heated and he dipped his head to suck at her breast.

"Oh, I love when you suck on my nipple. And you're getting hard inside me again."

He raised his head and grinned. "What do you expect when you tease your nipples like that?"

She squeezed him inside again.

He groaned. "And when you do that to my cock."

"Fuck me again, Shane," she murmured into his ear. "Make me come again."

"Whatever you want, honey."

He pulled her tight to his body and thrust into her. Again and again he drove deep and hard. She wrapped her legs around him and moaned. A second orgasm burst through her, exploding in a torrent of bliss.

"I'm coming. Oh, Master, I'm coming!"

Shane stiffened inside her, then burst into climax. She clung to him, holding him close, totally aware of what she'd just said.

Finally, he drew away from her.

"Master?" His eyebrow quirked up.

Her cheeks burned. "Well, you're . . . uh . . . master of my pleasure."

It was bad, but would he call her on it? As he stared at her, doubt clamoring in his eyes, she knew he wouldn't.

Thank heavens, because she had enough to worry about sorting out what they'd do about Kyle, without introducing her history with Max into the situation.

Max hung up the phone after leaving a message asking Summer to call him back. He wished Summer had answered her cell phone. He leaned back in his high-backed leather office chair and stared out his thirtieth-story window at the sun glinting off the office towers around him. He'd really wanted to hear her voice again.

God, this past weekend with her had been incredibly hot. He still remembered how she'd looked when he'd left her Sunday night . . . all dewy-eyed . . . soft and sexy . . . with the glow of a woman who'd been well loved.

But now he was back in his office in New York, and she was back at her job in Port Smith. Maybe she was with Shane and Kyle right now, having their coffee break. The two men she wanted to start a relationship with.

He glanced at the picture of Summer and Tanya from the Sex-à-la-Gala show displayed on the top right of his large computer monitor. Summer was such a beautiful woman, yet so withdrawn sexually. But she was definitely breaking out of herself. She was learning to express herself—even talk a little dirty.

He shook his head. She really needed to break out of her cocoon of safety . . . push past her comfort zone and go after what she wanted. She'd taken the first step on Friday night, and he hoped she'd try again.

Making love with Shane and Kyle would be good for her.

Unfortunately, a tiny prick of jealousy marred his sense of satisfaction. Which disturbed him. But it wasn't jealousy, it was just lust. The thought of her in the other men's arms with their cocks deep inside her made Max long for the same thing. That wasn't the same as jealousy. He *wanted* Summer to have sex with Shane. And Kyle. He liked the satisfaction of his sub growing and embracing what she wanted. His ultimate goal was her happiness.

Max's phone warbled. He picked up the receiver.

"Hello."

"Hi, Max."

He smiled at the sound of Summer's voice. "Summer. Thanks for calling me back. I just wanted to thank you for the wonderful weekend."

"Well, thank you for coming here," she murmured. "I had a great time."

He nodded, remembering the feel of her soft body in his arms.

"So have you run into Shane or Kyle this morning?" She'd been concerned about it being awkward when she saw them again, but he'd tried to convince her not to worry. The guys would probably ignore the whole incident.

"Yes, I . . . uh . . . saw Shane."

He smiled. "I see. It sounds like something interesting happened."

"Well, yes. I . . . ."

"Tell me about it," he prompted at her hesitation.

"Shane and I . . . in my office we . . . ."

He chuckled. "The two of you made out in your office? How was it?"

"It was . . . incredible."

His stomach tightened a little. It wasn't like him to get caught up in male pride like that. He knew his strengths, and he didn't feel threatened by the fact that another man had made his sub come. Max could make her come on command. Anyway, it wasn't a contest. He was thrilled that Summer had enjoyed her romp with Shane, and he hoped she would pursue Kyle now. She was attracted to both men, so she should have both men, even if she decided to continue a relationship with only one after the fact.

"That's good. Now what are you going to do about Kyle?"

"I'm not sure. I feel guilty that I've been with Shane. It's like I've chosen him over Kyle."

"There's an easy way to fix that. Go to Kyle's office now and seduce him."

Silence hung on the line.

"I . . . don't think I can do that."

He listened carefully to her tone. Hesitation. Uncertainty. But he was sure she wanted to. She just needed a little encouragement.

"Where are you now, Summer?"

"In my office."

"Shane is gone?"

"Yes."

"Would Kyle be in his office now?"

"Yes, I think so. He usually schedules quiet time in his office for a couple of hours every morning."

"So it's the perfect time."

Eleven

Kyle heard a tap on his door but ignored it. Whoever it was, Susan, his secretary, would shoo them away. These were his quiet work hours. No appointments. No interruptions.

The door opened and he glanced up. Summer popped her head in the door.

"Sorry to bother you."

He put down his pen and closed the folder with the monthly report from the catering department he'd been reviewing.

"It's all right," he said.

Her cheeks were tinged with red, and she hesitated.

"You're busy. Maybe I should come back later."

He stood up. "It's all right. Come in."

He'd intended to find a time to talk to her sometime today anyway. The fact that she'd come here now, knowing his routine, made him more than a little curious.

She stepped inside and closed the door behind her, then stepped toward him.

"Sit down." He gestured toward a chair by his round table, then sat beside her. "What's up?"

Her fingers toyed nervously with the top button of her blouse, but she said nothing.

"Is it about Friday night?" he prompted. Had she come here to gauge his reaction? To find out if he was angry?

She leaned back in her chair and took a deep breath, expanding her chest. An image of those luscious, rose-tipped breasts, which had haunted him since Friday night, sent heat rushing through him.

He took her hand. Her soft, delicate fingers were cold, so he cradled them between his.

"You know you can talk to me about anything, Summer. I won't judge."

She nodded and drew in another breath.

"That night was . . . strange. It's just that I've been wanting to . . ." She chewed her lower lip and gazed at him. "I've been attracted to you . . . and to Shane . . . for a long time, and I think it's time I do something about it. You told me on that day that . . . you are attracted to me."

Summer watched as Kyle's sea green eyes darkened to the color of moss.

"I am."

His solemn words sent her pulse racing. She leaned toward him, her heart pounding in her chest.

"Show me."

He stood up and dragged her to her feet. His lips captured hers before she had a chance to breathe. Passionate and compelling, his kiss devoured her. She wrapped her arms

around his broad shoulders, swept away by his passion, clinging to him for support. His hands slid down her back and
over her hips. He drew her toward him, tight against his
body . . . and his growing erection.

"Summer, you don't know how long I've waited for
this," Kyle murmured against her ear, then captured her lips
again.

"Don't wait any longer." She dragged her fingers around
his shirt collar, then down his button placket. She released
the first button.

His moss gaze captured hers. "You want to do this here?
Now?"

She pressed her lips to his neck, then nuzzled under his
chin, feeling his hot pulse racing under her lips.

"Yes." She took his hand and drew it to her breast.

Kyle cupped her firm, round flesh. Heat blazed through
him, and his groin pulsed with need at her softness . . . at
the sexy whimper of pleasure his touch elicited. At finally
satisfying the yearning to touch her so intimately. A yearning that had haunted his dreams for what seemed like ae-
ons.

"Tell me what to do." Her soft words rippled through
him.

His eyes narrowed. "Like in your friend's book?"

Her eyes widened. "You read Tanya's book?"

He smiled. "Why not? You seemed to enjoy it." He
stroked her breast. "So, you're interested in BDSM?"

"Her book . . . it was really about Domination and submission."

Had she developed a taste for kinky sex?

No, not kinky. In the book, it had been a loving give-

and-take, allowing the submissive to let go of control in order to fully realize her pleasure. And to grow.

That could be exactly what Summer needed . . . and he'd rather she get it from him than some big-city stranger who might hurt her.

"You want me to dominate you?" he asked.

The blue of her eyes deepened as she nodded.

The thought of it turns her on.

And that turned him on.

Summer loved the hot passion that had flared between her and Shane, but she had been missing the control Max exerted over her when he made love to her. Both Shane and Kyle were strong, confident men, but Kyle had a masterful side she longed to submit to.

He smiled, then stepped back and sent a lingering gaze down her body. Heat sizzled across her skin.

Then his smile faded and his eyes glinted like granite. Suddenly, he seemed forceful and overwhelmingly masculine.

"Open your blouse."

She hesitated.

"Open it *now*." The words, spoken in a low, commanding tone, sent her pulse racing. He seemed almost . . . dangerous.

But this was Kyle. A Kyle she'd never seen before, but still Kyle.

She released the first button of her blouse, then the next.

He growled, then strode forward and brushed her hands aside. He flicked open the buttons in record time, then shoved the blouse from her shoulders. It slipped to the ground before she had a chance to react, then he grabbed her wrists in his strong hands and walked her backward, as though he'd taken the lead on the dance floor. He stopped when her back pressed against the wall. He pushed her hands over her head, holding her pinned against the wall, then he took her lips in a potent assault. His tongue drove into her mouth, exploring her boldly.

She sucked in air as her heart thundered.

Kyle thrilled at the feel of Summer yielding to him. Her body melted against him as he plundered her mouth.

"Summer," he murmured in her ear. He stroked down her arms and caught her around the waist, then lifted her. "Wrap your legs around me."

She did it instantly. He carried her to his desk and sat her atop it, then he stepped back.

"Take off your bra," he demanded.

Her cheeks turned a deep rose.

"Do it," he insisted, authority sizzling through his voice.

"Yes, sir."

She tucked her arms behind her to unhook the bra.

"Slowly."

She nodded, then eased the strap off one side, letting it fall over her silky white shoulder, then she dropped the other strap. Her fingers tucked under the satin-and-lace cups, and she held the delicate cloth to her breasts for a moment, as though too shy to reveal them . . . then slowly eased the sexy garment away.

His breath caught at the sight of her beautiful, round naked breasts. The nipples, a dark rosy color, pushed forward to tight nubs as he stared at them.

"Get rid of the rest of your clothes. You have two seconds."

Summer stood up and her hands darted to her skirt zipper, and she tugged it down and thrust it over her hips. She pushed down her lacy panties before her skirt even hit the floor.

The threatening tone in Kyle's voice as he'd uttered the harsh command rocked through her, and she could barely breathe. The danger in his manner filled her with astonishing need.

Max had never spoken to her in such a threatening tone. Of course, if he had, she would have balked for sure. Kyle, on the other hand . . . She'd known him a long time, and . . . she trusted him completely.

She stepped out of her shoes and the pool of fabric surrounding them. Now she stood before him totally naked.

He nodded, and his glittering green gaze raked over her.

"Good. Now sit in my chair and open your legs."

She walked around his desk and sat in his big, leather chair, then opened her legs.

"Stroke yourself."

She stroked over her slit. Her slippery juices coated her fingers.

"Are you wet?"

"Yes, sir."

"Good."

He tugged on his belt, unfastening the buckle, then unzipped his pants. He kicked off his shoes, then pushed his pants to the floor and stepped toward her. He leaned against the desk beside her.

"Take out my cock."

She sucked in a breath.

"Yes, sir."

She had longed to see his big cock. To touch it. Now, she would finally get the chance.

She reached toward the bulge in his navy striped boxers and stroked over it lovingly, then she slipped her hand inside the opening.

"It's so hard."

She drew it out and admired the rigid shaft of male muscle. Almost as long as Shane's, but thicker. The bulbous head oozed a clear drop of liquid.

"I didn't say you could talk." His flare of anger seemed almost real. "You only talk in response to a question or an order. Do you understand?"

She lowered her head. "Yes, sir."

"Good. Now suck my cock."

She leaned forward and opened her mouth over his thick cock head. She drew him in slowly, first covering the corona, then gliding her lips down his shaft. She opened her throat and swallowed him whole, then eased back.

"Suck it."

She sucked on him, squeezing him within her mouth, drawing on him hard. His hands stroked through her hair, then tightened as he drew her head back.

"That's good. Too good."

He drew his cock from her mouth.

"Stand up."

"Yes, sir."

He stood up, too, and grasped her around the waist with his big, strong hands and lifted her onto the desk. He pressed her thighs apart, spreading her legs wide, and stepped forward, then invaded her mouth. She gasped at his potent masculinity. His hands cupped her head as his tongue plunged deep into her mouth.

He drew back, his face only inches from hers.

"I'm going to fuck you now."

His hard, emerald eyes held her gaze, gauging. When she did not protest, he shifted his pelvis forward and she felt his cock head press against her wet opening. His hands wrapped around her hips and he pulled her against him, driving his cock inside her in one deep, forceful stroke. Her body welcomed him, her vagina clenching around him in uncontrollable need. She almost wailed at the intensity of it.

Embedded deeply inside her, he leaned forward and took one hard nipple into his mouth and twirled his tongue over the nub. Her fingers raked through his thick, wavy hair, and she whimpered. He drew the nipple into his mouth and nipped it lightly with his teeth. She cried out at the intense pleasure-pain sensation.

He began sucking, lightly at first, then hard. What had been a whimper turned to a moan.

He swept the papers and files on his desktop sideways and flattened his hand on her chest, pushing her down until she lay beneath him on the desk. He grabbed her wrists and held them over her head.

He nipped her nipple, then drew back and thrust his cock into her again.

She moaned, tears welling in her eyes at the intensity of the pleasure.

"Do you like me fucking you, Summer?"

"Yes, sir."

He thrust again, even deeper this time.

"Oh, God, yes." She sucked in air, her head spinning. Tears streamed from her eyes. "Please, sir. Make me come."

He tucked both her wrists into one powerful hand and slid the other over her breast and pinched her nipple. She gasped. He stroked down her stomach, then slid his fingers into her folds, right above his cock as he drove it into her again. He found her clit and swirled over it.

Red hot pleasure flared through her, and she moaned as an orgasm ripped through her. He continued to plunge into her. Just as her spike of pleasure subsided, he increased his pumping and flicked her clit again. Another, more powerful surge of bliss blazed through her.

"Oh, God, yes!" She gasped for air as she plummeted into infinity, her body singed with white heat.

His cock thrust deeper and he stiffened, then convulsed into her. Hot liquid seared her insides, filling her with satisfaction.

She'd pleased him.

His cock twitched within her as they both caught their breath. As reality slowly returned, she found herself staring up at . . .

Kyle.

During their lovemaking, he'd become someone else. Someone powerful and exciting. She'd always been attracted to him, but she'd had no idea how potently erotic he could be.

But now he was Kyle again. Her cheeks burned as he stared down at her, his cock still hard within her.

"Don't tell me you're going to turn bashful now?"

"No, sir."

He grinned. "If you keep that up, I'll have to turn you over my knee."

Her eyes widened and her vagina clenched at the thought.

His grin widened. "Why, Summer, you'd like that, wouldn't you?"

Before she could react, he drove into her again. She gasped, then felt the waves of pleasure rise once more. He pumped into her, forcing the waves higher, until she clung to him in another mind-shattering orgasm.

His gaze remained locked on her face as she wailed in release. Finally, she slumped back on the desk, sucking in air.

"So, tell me, Summer. Are you going to continue to fuck both Shane and me separately? Or should we go right to a threesome?"

Twelve

Kyle could see the panic in Summer's widened eyes.

"I . . . uh . . ." She glanced around as though trapped.

He had hoped by making the bold statement, she would feel more comfortable moving to the next step, which she obviously wanted—a ménage à trois with him and Shane. The mere thought sent his wilting cock, still encased in her warm, wet sheath, throbbing to life.

He hadn't known she'd made love to Shane, but guilt clearly laced her features. After seeing her kiss Shane last week, then her behavior Friday night, he'd been thinking a lot about the relationship among the three of them and had come to the conclusion that they could handle a threesome. In fact, the thought of seeing Summer being fucked by Shane, of driving his own cock into her while Shane thrust into her, too, set his blood boiling.

He pulled her against his body and lifted her from the desk. He stormed her sweet lips with his as he moved toward the wall, then pressed her against it as he drove his hard, pulsing cock deep into her. She tightened her legs around him and moaned as he pulled back and thrust into her again.

He pounded faster and faster until they both erupted in yet another orgasm.

On Friday morning, Summer sipped her coffee as she sat with Kyle and Shane at the sunny table by the window. Shane ate his sandwich, and Kyle stared out the window.

Four days ago, when Kyle had asked her about a three-some, she'd been totally freaked out and wanted some time to figure out if she really wanted that to be their next step.

Since then, she didn't like how awkward it felt when the three of them were together. The easy time they'd once shared over coffee in the morning had become tense . . . at least for her.

She glanced at Kyle, then Shane. The fact was, she was in love with both of them. It looked as though she'd been right to fear that a romantic entanglement could threaten their friendship. Now she wasn't sure if she should pull back on her intimate relationship with each of them or go full speed ahead into a three-way.

Carol stopped by the table with a coffeepot in her hand and filled Summer's cup, then leaned toward Summer and nudged her arm.

"Did you see the hunk at table fifty-two? We don't see that kind of tall, handsome fella around here too often."

Summer glanced toward the second table by the window. Her heart lurched.

Max!

What was he doing here?

He glanced her way and smiled. Oh, God, was he going to come over here? But no, he just picked up his coffee and took a sip, watching her.

She jerked her gaze to her coffee cup and the packet of sugar in her hand. She ripped it open and dumped it into her cup, then poured in some cream and stirred vigorously.

Carol filled Shane's cup, then Kyle's.

Summer's gaze drifted back to Max. She still couldn't get over how good-looking he was. Glossy ebony hair worn in a short, spiky style, longer on top than at the sides. He wore black jeans and his black leather jacket over a white shirt open over a black T-shirt. The sunlight from the window caught on the diamond stud in his ear.

"You know him?" Shane asked, his keen gaze on her.

"No." She sipped her coffee.

She wasn't sure why she'd lied, except that if she hadn't, it would have led to the inevitable question of where she'd met him, and if she said at the Sex-à-la-Gala show, then somehow she felt Shane would figure it all out. Things were already complicated enough.

She felt Kyle's gaze burning along her neck, and she wondered if he knew.

Oh, man, why had Max come here?

Max opened his wallet and dropped some bills on the table. He was about to leave. She hoped he wouldn't come over here.

Summer pushed herself to her feet.

"I've got to go." The words sounded too abrupt, but she couldn't take them back.

Shane and Kyle stared at her.

"I . . . uh . . . have some stuff I have to get done."

She grabbed her purse from the chair beside her and headed toward the door. Quickly. It was a lame excuse, but she didn't care. She was more concerned with getting out of there before Max got to the table and introduced himself.

Shane watched Summer race out the door. "What the hell's gotten into her?"

The tall man she'd exchanged a sultry look with exited the restaurant.

"I think she's trying to avoid the guy." Kyle sipped his coffee.

"She did seem pretty skittish."

"Think that's the guy she met at the show?"

Shane was silent for a moment. "I'm not sure. But clearly he's trouble."

Summer strode into her store and nodded at Cindy as she headed into her office and closed the door behind her.

A moment later, Cindy poked her head in.

"There's someone here who'd like to speak with the manager."

Summer stood up, knowing exactly who it would be. She stepped to the door and there stood Max.

"Thanks, Cindy." She turned to Max. "Please come in."

A moment later, Max followed her across the room to her desk.

"What are you doing here?" she asked, keeping her voice low. She would not close the door. She didn't close the door with visitors, and she didn't want to draw any more attention to Max than his good looks and charismatic presence did all on their own.

"I wanted to see you."

Her heart swelled at his words—she had missed Max so much. But things with Shane and Kyle were already complicated enough. How could she deal with Max, too?

"Because I wanted to touch you." He stepped closer, and anticipation thrummed through her. He stroked his hand over her shoulder—bare except for the narrow strap of her white camisole top and the powder blue strap of her bra—sending the delicate hairs prickling to attention.

"Because I wanted to do this." His lips brushed her neck, and she jolted back a step.

She couldn't afford to let him touch her, to allow herself to fall under his seductive spell. Not here.

She took a step to the right to peer through the office door. Cindy was busy with a customer.

"Don't look so nervous. I'm not going to do anything to embarrass you." He smiled. "And I know you're moving forward with your relationship with Kyle and Shane, but . . . I wanted to see you one more time. Spend one last weekend with you."

"But . . . I can't just—"

He smiled and stroked her cheek. "I'm sure you can."

A couple of days with Max. In the flesh. Her stomach quivered in anticipation.

She heard a sound and glanced toward the door, but no one was there.

"I can't just leave with no explanation."

"You're the owner. You must have someone you can hand the reigns to. And as the owner, you don't need to give explanations."

Cindy was a great assistant. She'd be able to handle anything that came up on the weekend, and this afternoon shouldn't be too busy.

He grinned. "Am I going to have to tie you up?"

Tie her up? Her breath caught in her lungs.

The realization hit Summer like a punch in the gut. Max was giving her one more weekend with him and then she'd never see him again. She couldn't let this opportunity slip away.

"I . . . uh . . . would need to go home and pick up some things."

"That won't be necessary." The glint in his eye told her a nightgown wouldn't be required. "Where is your car?"

"It's parked in the lot by the tennis courts. It's a blue Corolla."

He nodded and held out his hand. "Give me your keys and I'll meet you there in ten minutes."

She opened her desk drawer and fished around in her purse, then handed the keys to him.

He left the office, and she heard the little bell over the door as he left the store.

She sucked in a deep breath and grabbed the powder blue linen jacket she'd left hanging over the back of her chair and draped it over her arm, then plucked her purse from her desk drawer and headed to the door.

"Cindy, I'm going to take the rest of the day off and I'll be away for the weekend. Can you be on call if the staff needs anything?"

Cindy stared at her, her lips pressed tight. "Sure. How long will you be gone?"

Summer hesitated. "Uh . . . assume until Monday. I'll call if plans change."

As Summer pushed open the door, Cindy said, "Summer . . ."

Summer turned. The look of concern on her young assistant's face surprised her.

"What is it, Cindy?"

"Is everything okay?"

Summer smiled reassuringly. "Of course. I just decided to take a couple of days off and enjoy the beautiful summer weather."

As Summer stepped toward her car, she saw that Max sat in the driver's seat.

She glanced around to ensure no one was watching, then pulled open the passenger door and slipped inside. She turned and placed her purse and jacket on the backseat. He smiled, then started the car and drove from the parking lot. They pulled onto the highway about ten minutes later. When they were about five miles from the hotel on a quiet stretch of road, Max pulled onto the shoulder. Once the car stopped, he turned toward her.

"Now, to get this adventure off to the right start . . ." He leaned closer. "Did you miss me?"

She nodded, anticipating his lips on hers. He didn't disappoint. He captured her lips and drew her into his arms in a sweet, poignant kiss. She loved being in his arms again, the heat of his body warming her.

"Damn, I've missed you," he murmured.

His spicy, musky male scent enveloped her, and she sighed as she stared at his glimmering gray eyes.

"Me too."

His broad smile revealed his dazzling white teeth. "Good. Now take off your top."

Her eyes widened. "But . . . I can't sit here . . . like that . . ." She didn't want to say in only her bra because she knew where that would lead.

"Summer, show me how much you trust me. Take off your top."

He could have ordered her. He must have known by now that would work. But he didn't. He'd asked her to trust him.

She pulled the white camisole over her head. His gaze rested on her powder blue bra. He brushed his fingertip along the scalloped lace at the top of the cup. Tingles danced along her skin at the feel of his warm touch.

"Very pretty." His finger slipped under the strap. "Now take this off, too."

Her eyes widened, but she reached behind her and unfastened the hooks, then peeled the bra away. His smile widened.

He took her top and bra and tossed them onto the backseat, then handed her a folded white top. She lifted it up. It was a thin white tank top.

"Put it on."

She pulled it over her head and over her torso, covering her breasts, then tucked it in. It actually went very nicely with the blue-and-white paisley print of her full skirt.

She glanced down at herself. Her nipples showed clearly through the thin white cotton, and the shirt hugged her breasts. Not a lot was left to the imagination, but she wasn't naked—and other drivers wouldn't notice.

Max stroked over her left breast, and delicious sensations rippled through her.

"Now take off your panties."

She reached under her full skirt and shimmied out of her panties, also powder blue, then handed them to him. He tossed those onto the backseat as she smoothed down her skirt.

"Now, to fully set us in the mood for our little adventure . . ." He leaned past her, his arms brushing against her breast, and drew a rope from under her seat.

"Hold out your wrists."

She glanced at the rope, then at him, and licked her lips, then complied. He took the rope and wrapped it around one wrist and then the other. He coiled it around a few more times, twisted, looped, then pulled it tight. She sucked in a quick breath at the intense excitement that spiked through her at the feel of the binding cord biting into her flesh. Not that he'd made it too tight . . . it just made her feel . . . dominated. . . .

"Now, think about the fact that I've kidnapped you and you are totally at my mercy. Think about what will happen to you when I get you to that cabin."

Her blood heated at the thought. Maybe he would tear off her clothes. He would probably tie her up. She would be helpless against his demands.

Unless she used her safe word. Which was highly un-likely!

Her vagina clenched. She and Max would be together tonight. She could hardly wait to see that long, thick cock of his again. To feel it against her lips. To feel it moving inside her, bringing her to an incredible orgasm. She wouldn't let herself think about how much she'd miss him when he was gone.

As they drove, he reached under the thin fabric and stroked her breasts, paying attention to one for several minutes, then the other. After a while, his hand slipped to the hem of her skirt and slid underneath. The whole time, his gaze remained fixed on the road. She felt his warm fingers glide up her inner thigh.

"Open your legs."

She shifted one foot to open the gap between her thighs. His finger slipped to her folds, then slid between. He tucked his finger inside, then swirled lightly. He slid another finger inside, then left them there while he continued to drive. Need built within her as his fingertips remained there, nestled inside her, unmoving. She shifted in her seat, wanting to feel them moving inside her.

He chuckled. "Sit still. It's another hour's drive. We have plenty of time to enjoy the journey."

She arched her breasts forward and dropped her head against the headrest, her eyelids closing. She wanted him to stroke her and bring her to orgasm. This was going to be the longest ride of her life.

Thirteen

Shane sipped his coffee as Kyle reviewed the recommendations section of Shane's report analyzing new electronic security systems for the hotel. They'd spent the last hour going over the numbers, trying to find the most cost-effective solution.

A knock sounded at the door. Shane glanced at his watch. It was after five-thirty, and Susan, Kyle's secretary, would have gone home by now.

"Come in," Kyle said.

The door opened and Cindy popped her head in the door.

"Shane. I've been looking for you. I need to talk to you." She glanced at Kyle. "Sorry to interrupt. It's about Summer."

Kyle nodded and returned to the report, but Shane knew he'd be listening intently. Shane stood up and walked to the door.

"What is it, Cindy?" he asked.

"I tried to find you earlier, but . . ."

"I was at another client site."

She nodded. "Well, it might be nothing, but . . . I'm afraid Summer might be in some kind of trouble."

He gripped the edge of the door. "Why do you think that?"

"There was this guy who came into the shop this morning. He was in her office, and I heard part of their conversation. I don't usually listen to her stuff, but he seemed kind of intimidating and . . ."

Alarm bells clanged in his head. The guy in the coffee shop this morning.

"What did you hear?" Kyle said as he approached the door.

"I think he was threatening her."

Shane's gut clenched.

"Exactly what did he say?" Kyle asked.

"Well, I don't remember exactly, but he insisted she go somewhere with him. She wanted to go home and get some stuff, but he wouldn't let her, and . . ."

"What else, Cindy?" Shane asked when her words faded.

"He threatened to tie her up." She gazed at him with wide eyes. "It was chilling how he said it. So calm. As if he did that kind of thing all the time."

Summer stared at the big country house as Max parked on the curved driveway in front. This was Tanya's family's house—actually, Tanya's now that her mother had died and left it to her. Tanya kept it, even though she didn't live here, saying maybe she'd move here someday, but it seemed clear that she just wasn't ready to let go. In the meantime, she rented it out, mostly to summer vacationers. It was on five acres of land, had a barn off to one side, and afforded access to a beautiful lake. Her family used to keep a couple of horses. Summer remembered coming up here a few times when she was a teenager and they'd taken the horses out on woodland trails and on a gorgeous path along the lakeshore.

Max opened her door and tucked his fingers around her elbow to help her from the car, then led her into the house. The large living room with the huge stone fireplace had updated furniture from what Summer remembered, soft beige sofas with earth-tone cushions and large paintings on the walls. Her heels clacked on the hardwood floor.

Max slid his arm around her waist and tugged her against his body, facing him. His hard, muscular chest greeted her soft breasts. Her nipples pressed against him through the thin fabric of the tank top.

"You are my captive. No matter how much you fight, you cannot escape."

So he had set the scene for this evening. She should fight him, to make the scenario more realistic . . . and she suspected he would not want her to call him Master, since it wouldn't fit the role.

"Why have you kidnapped me?" she asked in an anxious voice.

His fingers forked through her hair, then he nuzzled behind her ear. "Why do you think?"

She pulled away from him as much as she could with his arm snugly around her waist.

"No, you can't do this."

He cupped his hand around her head, and his mouth dropped to hers. His tongue forced its way into her mouth, and he stroked boldly, then withdrew, leaving her breathless.

"I can and I will."

He scooped her up and carried her up the stairs, then through a door to a bedroom. He tossed her onto the bed, then sat beside her and worked at the rope tying her wrists together. She waited patiently, like a good captive, while he freed her hands, waiting for an opportunity to attempt escape. He unwrapped the rope, and as the final loop released, she tried to bolt from the bed, but he grabbed her wrists. She gasped as he forced her flat on the bed, then climbed over her, pinning her between his strong thighs. He stared down at her, a fierce smile on his face.

He produced black straps from the bedside table and wrapped one around her left wrist and snapped it tight, then fastened the other around her right wrist. He shoved aside one of the pillows to reveal a clasp attached to a strap that disappeared under the bed. With a flick of his thumb, he attached the clasp to a metal ring on the wrist strap, then did the same with her other wrist.

His hands slid under her body and she felt the waistband of her skirt release, then he slid the zipper down. He pushed himself off the bed and tugged her skirt down her legs, then off, leaving her lower body naked. He grabbed more straps from the bedside table, then bound and fastened her ankles just as he had her wrists.

She was now spread-eagled on the bed, wearing only the thin tank top. Not even panties. He left the room through a different door from the one they'd entered, and she heard water running. A moment later, he returned with a glass of water. He took a sip as he stared at her, his gaze gliding along her body, scrutinizing every part of her with great interest. Suddenly, he flicked the glass toward her, and cold water drenched her chest. Her nipples puckered instantly. The white fabric became basically transparent. He chuckled and turned to leave.

"No, let me go," she wailed, throwing herself against her restraints.

He turned back to face her.

"Let me go right now," she demanded.

He stepped toward her and sat on the bed. Was he going to do it?

He tugged a gag from his jacket pocket. As he brought it toward her face, she tossed her head from side to side, but he clamped his hand around her chin and forced it into her mouth, then attached the straps.

She watched as he walked out the door, leaving her helpless . . . gagged . . . *and totally turned on.*

She was very conscious of her arms spread wide over her head. The wet fabric stretched across her cold, hard nipples. Her legs were wide open, the moisture pooling inside.

Oh, man, she wanted Max—her captor—to come back and climb on top of her, force his huge cock inside her, then ride her until she wailed in release.

But he didn't.

She lay there as the room darkened around her with the setting sun, helpless and vulnerable, imagining all the sexy things Max could do to her in this position.

The smell of cooking—onions and chicken—set her mouth watering. She'd been lying bound to the bed for about an hour when he finally returned with a plate of food. He pulled a chair forward and sat down, then rested his feet on the bed beside her. He watched her as he ate. Her mouth watered around the gag in her mouth. When he finished, he left the room, but to her relief, he returned with another plate of food.

"Be nice and I'll remove the gag."

She nodded, and he unbuckled the strap at the back of her head. She thought he'd unfasten her hands, but he didn't. Instead, he held a fork with a small morsel of chicken to her lips. She ate it, savoring the delicious, spicy flavor. He intended to feed her, and he'd cut the meat into small pieces so she wouldn't choke. He fed her over the next fifteen minutes, then set aside the plate. He brought another glass of water from the bathroom, and she cringed in anticipation of the cold assault, assuming he'd fling the water at her again—her tank top had dried—but he slid his hand behind her head and lifted, then placed the water to her lips. She sipped several times, then he placed the water on the bedside table.

He dipped several fingers into the water and smeared them over her nipple. It spiked against the fabric.

"Lovely." He wet the other one, too, then stroked over both hard, wet nipples. The exquisite sensation rippled through her, sending her hormones skyrocketing.

She wanted him to touch her now. Everywhere. To kiss her. Taste her.

He squeezed her nipples, then pinched them. She arched upward.

"You're a very cooperative captive."

Remembering her role, she flung her body to one side, as much as the restraints allowed, then flung the other way, jarring his fingers free. He climbed on top of her, his sexy, hot body pinning her down. He held her head and kissed her neck, then sat up again. He palmed her breasts, then stroked and squeezed them to his heart's content, despite her protests, sprinkled with moans of pleasure at the tingles radiating through her body.

He pushed himself off the bed and divested himself of his shirt and pants. She watched avidly as he pushed his underwear down, revealing his lovely cock. She licked her lips but widened her eyes as if in alarm. He settled on top of her again, pinning her between his knees. He rocked forward and back, his hard, hot shaft gliding between her soft breasts. He pressed them together so they cradled his cock in their warmth.

She watched as his cock head pushed forward from between her breasts, then disappeared again. He released her breasts, and this time his cock slid forward until it brushed her lips. She flung her head to one side, rejecting his cock, even though she longed for it in her mouth.

He grasped her head and steadied it, then fed his cock into her mouth. Now impaled with his huge shaft, his broad cock head filling her mouth, she wondered how to pleasure him while staying in character.

"Suck it and maybe I'll let you go."

Good enough!

She licked his cock head, stroking her tongue over the tip, then around the base of the corona. She squeezed him in her mouth, then began to suck. He eased forward a little, then back, easing in and out as she squeezed him in her mouth. Then he tensed and thrust forward. She licked and squeezed, then sucked hard. He groaned, then erupted into her mouth.

He smiled and slid down her body, his cock falling from her mouth. He knelt between her knees and stared at her open legs. He leaned down and his tongue licked over her slit, then tunneled inside her.

She should arch and struggle, but she didn't want to. His fingers slipped inside her and she moaned. He licked her clit and pleasure spiked through her. He teased and cajoled. She gasped, feeling an orgasm closing in on her. Closer. Closer.

He drew back and chuckled, then shifted off the bed.

"No," she wailed as he left the room.

She arched and wiggled her hips, trying to find some relief from the intense need he'd built in her. She wanted him inside her. She wanted an orgasm.

He returned about a half hour later and leaned over her, tugged the neckline of her top under her breasts, baring them, then grasped a nipple in his mouth. He sucked and she arched against him, all pretense at struggling against him gone. He licked and teased while his hand found her other nipple and teased it, too.

She arched her hips. "Oh, God, please fuck me."

He laughed. "I thought you wanted me to let you go."

Summer groaned but forced herself back into character.

"I do. What I said was, 'Oh, God, please don't fuck me.'"

Max climbed over her, and she watched him stroke his huge, erect cock.

"Oh, is that what you said. Funny, I was sure you begged me to fuck you."

He placed his cock head to her sopping wet slit.

"No." She shook her head, loving the feel of his cock head gliding along her slit. "Please stop. Don't do this."

"What? Don't do this?" He thrust forward, impaling her with his cock. Stretching her with his immense girth.

She wailed.

He drew back and thrust again, filling her to the hilt.

He captured her nipple in his mouth and sucked hard, making her moan, then he drew back and thrust again.

Pleasure careened through her. He began a steady rhythm of thrusts. Deep. Increasing in speed. Waves of intense bliss flooded her senses.

"Oh, yeah. I'm going to . . ." Her insides pulsed and she plunged off the edge. "I'm coming!" Her voice rose in a trill, then she gasped as ecstasy claimed her.

Max tensed and hot liquid filled her as her voice trailed away in a moan.

They both lay gasping for air as their pulses slowly returned to normal. Max nuzzled her neck.

"You were absolutely fabulous." He grinned at her. "You're the best captive I've ever had."

Summer smiled, surprised at how much those words meant to her.

Max released Summer from her bonds, and they took a shower together, then they snuggled in bed with a nice fire blazing in the bedroom fireplace. He enjoyed the delicate mango scent of her hair, the silky feel of her skin against his cheek, the softness of her body pressed the length of his.

He didn't usually sleep with his subs. Once the sex was done, either he or his partner would return home or to their own hotel rooms if they were out of town. He hadn't wanted to sleep with a woman since Elena—God, he still missed her so much—but Summer was different from his other subs. Softer, more vulnerable. He loved having her in his bed.

When he'd met her—he couldn't believe it had been only two short weeks ago—she had been so afraid of her own desires, yet with the courage to step forward and follow her heart . . . and try something radically new for her. It had been exciting and refreshing introducing her to the rigors of Dominance and submission. And showing her the ropes, so to speak, of bondage and discipline had been highly stimulating for both of them.

She murmured softly, and he realized she'd fallen asleep. He nuzzled her temple, breathing in her sweet scent. He loved being the one to widen her perceptions of love and sex . . . and to help her expand her sex life to encompass her deepest desires.

For her to go forward, he knew she'd need to let go of some of her limiting patterns of behavior. He glanced into the fire and tried to figure out the best strategy to help Summer.

Shane's fingers gripped the steering wheel tightly as he drove along the sunny country road.

"You're driving a little fast, buddy," Kyle said from the passenger's seat.

Shane didn't need to glance at the speedometer. He knew he was close to twenty over the limit. He eased off the gas pedal. Getting there dead wouldn't help Summer.

"Don't think the worst," Kyle said. "At least we know who she's with and where to find her."

Before they'd left, Kyle had gotten in touch with Summer's friend Tanya to find out if the guy she'd disappeared with matched the description of her one-night stand from Chicago. Tanya had assured them that everything was fine. The man had whisked Summer away to Tanya's house in the country for a romantic getaway.

"This guy sounds like a stalker to me," said Shane. "You

heard what Cindy said. Who orders someone to go on a weekend getaway? I think Summer's gotten herself mixed up with a real creep."

"I don't know what's going on with her, Shane. Summer seems to be experimenting. Let's just wait until we get there to see what's going on."

The turnoff to Tanya's place was ahead. Shane made the right turn and followed the winding road the mile or so until they came to the big house with the barn off to the side.

There sat Summer's car.

Shane shoved open his car door and got out. His gut clenched at the sound of screams coming from the barn. Shane dodged forward, and Kyle raced after him.

Fourteen

Shane pulled open the old barn door a crack and peered inside. With his heart pounding in his chest, he wanted to race inside, but he needed to know what he was barreling into first. It was darker inside the barn than it was outside, so he could just make out two shapes. One smaller figure, arms stretched upward, and a taller, broader form. The larger figure's arm swung back, then flicked forward as though casting a fishing line . . . or cracking a whip.

Summer screamed.

Shane shoved the barn door all the way open and raced toward the man who was clearly whipping Summer. The guy stared at Shane in surprise, holding the whip, which had multiple tails.

The bastard!

Shane's fist slammed hard into the guy's jaw. He reeled backward, then wrapped his hand around his chin. Shane stepped forward to hit him again, but Kyle grabbed his arm and pulled him back.

"Shane, knock it off."

Shane jerked his arm free. "What the hell are you talking about? He's *beating* Summer."

"Shane? Kyle? What's happening?"

Now that his eyes had adjusted to the light, Shane could see that Summer's arms were stretched straight up with ropes attached around her wrists and tied to the rafters above.

She couldn't see what was happening. Not only were they behind her and she couldn't turn around, but a slender black blindfold, tied at the back of her head, covered her eyes. He glanced at her white tank top and, thankfully, didn't see any blood from the bastard's flogging.

"Shane and I heard your screams." Kyle strode in front of her.

As soon as he saw her hanging from the ceiling, the tank top scooped under her bare breasts, Kyle's groin tightened so painfully that he wanted to tear off her skirt and ravage her on the spot.

She quirked an eyebrow, visible above the shiny black cloth of the blindfold. "All the way from Port Smith? I wasn't yelling that loudly."

He smiled. As he'd suspected, she wasn't the victim of kidnapping—she and this guy were playing at bondage.

Now to convince Shane.

"We were worried about you," Shane said, glaring at the other guy, who wisely held back a couple of yards.

"Did you hit Max?" she asked, concern clear in her voice.

Kyle gazed at Shane, leaving him to answer.

"He was hurting you. Of course I hit him."

"Shane, I know you must have been worried about me, otherwise you wouldn't have followed me here, but Max didn't do anything wrong."

"He ties you to the ceiling and whips you and you say he didn't do anything wrong?"

"The whip doesn't hurt. It's soft suede, and he wasn't flogging hard. And I let him tie me up."

"Damn it, Summer. What the hell have you gotten into?" Kyle saw her cheeks blaze bright red.

"Shane, cool it. There's nothing wrong with experimenting with different sexual scenarios. Don't judge Summer."

Shane dragged his gaze from the tall stranger and glanced from Summer to Kyle, then released a breath.

He walked around her suspended form to face her. "Summer, I didn't mean to—"

The second he saw her ripe breasts pressing forward over her tank top, his words stopped abruptly. He stared at her hard nipples.

"Shane?" The red of Summer's face deepened.

He tugged his gaze from her round, delectable breasts to her face.

"Sorry, sweetie, I'm not judging you. I was just . . . worried about you."

She nodded.

Kyle knew they should offer to untie her, or at least remove the blindfold, but the sight of her hanging there helpless, her breasts visible and clearly wanting attention, made it impossible to think clearly.

"He wasn't hurting me. He was helping me release pent-up tension by having me scream. The whip is just a prop in a role-playing situation to help me. It's hard to just scream, you need to . . . build up to it somehow."

"So he tied you up and whipped you so you would scream to release stress?" Kyle asked.

The tall, black-haired man—Max Delaney was his name, according to Tanya—stepped forward but remained behind Summer, giving them all space.

"Not stress. Deeply held tension from long ago that has created patterns of limiting behavior."

"Like what?" Kyle asked, intrigued.

"Like not going after what I want," Summer answered, "because I'm afraid of taking risks."

Delaney quirked an eyebrow, then his gaze moved from Kyle to Shane and back again. Kyle got it immediately, but he did not see the dawn of understanding on Shane's face.

"Could I talk to you two outside?" Delaney moved toward them.

Shane glared at the guy, but Kyle nodded.

"Summer, we'll only be a short distance away," Delaney said. "If you need me, just call out and I'll hear you."

She nodded. Kyle followed Shane and Delaney out of the barn. Once they were far enough away that Summer wouldn't be able to hear them, Delaney turned toward them.

"Summer needs to feel she's in control—of her environment and of her life. That's why she's afraid to take risks."

"Don't tell *us* about Summer," Shane flared. "We've known her forever. You're just—"

Kyle gripped Shane's forearm. "Shane, hear him out." He turned back to face Delaney. "If she likes to be in control so much, why does she let you tie her up . . . and dominate her?"

Secret Ties

"A lot of people who need control in their lives like to give it up in a safe environment with someone they trust."

Shane glared at Delaney again. Anger and hurt simmered through him at the fact that Summer had trusted a virtual stranger over him.

"Most of the women I know who like to be dominated have high-powered, stressful jobs where they have to make a lot of decisions," Delaney continued. "Summer is different. She wants to control her environment to feel she's safe. She limits herself by only doing those things she knows she can succeed at. That she knows won't cause failure or problems of any kind."

"Why the hell are you talking to us about this?" Shane demanded. He hated hearing this stranger talk about Summer as if he'd known her for years.

"Because one of the things she wants is *you*." He turned to Kyle. "And you, too."

"We know that," Shane said.

"Do you understand that she wants you both *at the same time?*"

Shane's eyebrows rose, and he turned to Kyle.

"If you two are agreeable," Delaney said, "why don't you let her know right now?" He smiled. "She's just hanging around doing nothing at the moment."

Shane's fists clenched at his sides. "We're not going to do anything while she's tied up like that."

"Why not?" Kyle asked, his mouth turned up in a grin.

What the hell was up with Kyle? He seemed to be taking all of this pretty calmly.

Then Shane remembered when Summer had asked him

161

if he had handcuffs. His cock had swelled then, and it swelled now. She liked being bound. Damn, his sweet little Summer had a definite kinky side.

Summer heard the clunk of heels on the wood floor of the barn as someone walked toward her from behind . . . closer . . . until he stood behind her. She could feel his heat. Anticipation quivered through her.

"Max?"

Big, warm hands slid over her hips and drew her back against a hard, masculine body. A whisker-roughened face caressed her cheek, then nuzzled the crook of her neck, sending quivers through her.

"Shane."

Another hand grasped her top and jerked away, ripping the fabric down the front. She gasped. Cool air wafted across her naked torso as the tattered fabric flapped open.

She hadn't realized someone stood in front of her. Was it Max or Kyle?

From behind her, Shane's hands stroked around her ribs and cupped her breasts. The man in front of her grasped her jaw and his mouth captured hers. His masterful lips moved against hers, and his tongue glided inside. Max?

Shane's fingers stroked her nipples, triggering ripples of need, while Max's tongue danced with hers. No, not Max. The way he curled around her tongue, the way his thumbs stroked her temple while he cupped her face . . . This was Kyle.

Kyle's mouth released hers, and a second later she felt one of Shane's hands slip away from her breast, replaced by Kyle's mouth on her nipple.

"Kyle. It's you."

It was strange and exciting feeling them touch her in the darkness. Feeling their hands on her . . . their lips . . . but not being able to see them.

"What do you think of the idea of two of us making love to you?" Kyle asked.

"I . . . uh . . . like the idea." She swallowed. "A lot."

"You're practically naked," Shane murmured, "and we're going to ravage you." He nuzzled her ear. "What is your safe word?"

She sucked in a breath at the image. "Cat."

He chuckled, then both men moved away. Now she could hear the lighter sound of Kyle's shoes—probably the light deck shoes he often wore after hours in the summer.

"Look here, Kyle. A pretty little thing just hanging around waiting for us."

Summer tugged on the ropes holding her hands high in the air.

"What do you want?" she demanded.

Kyle ignored her words. "I think she'd look even prettier if we could see more of her."

His hands worked at her skirt, and she struggled against him, adrenaline rushing through her, adding to her excitement. The skirt fell from her body.

"No. Stop."

Shane's fingers slid under the elastic at her waist and rolled her thong downward, then off her feet.

"Don't do this," she said as she struggled against the ropes holding her arms stretched above her. She could feel her breasts bouncing with her movements and could almost feel the heat of their gazes watching.

Shane chuckled.

"Very nice." His hand reached around her and stroked one breast, then cupped it in his big hand.

"No." She struggled against him, and he tightened an arm around her waist and pulled her back against his hard body.

Kyle moved forward and wrapped his hands around her hips, then pressed his body tight against her, crushing her against Shane.

The heat of both their bodies . . . hard and muscled . . . pressing against her . . . took her breath away.

Kyle kissed one side of her neck while Shane nuzzled the other. She sucked in air, working hard not to succumb to the overwhelming sensations and simply melt into them. The roles they were playing were too exciting to abandon.

She wriggled between them, which thrust her puckered nipples hard into Kyle's chest and alternately pressed each of their bulging cocks into her soft body.

"For not wanting us to fuck you, you really are helping our cocks get hard," Kyle murmured.

She stopped moving, even though she wanted to feel both their cocks against her. Patience would bring greater rewards.

Shane's hands grasped the tattered remains of her top, and he ripped it from her body. Kyle grasped one nipple in his mouth and cupped her other breast, squeezing firmly. She heard a zipper, and a moment later, Shane's hot, naked cock pressed against her behind. He pulled her against his body and nuzzled her neck while Kyle slipped away. Another zipper sound, then his hot hands returned, stroking her breasts. Shane's hands grasped her around the waist and lifted her.

Kyle, who had crouched down, lifted her legs and tucked them over his shoulders, opening her legs wide. When his warm mouth pressed between her thighs and he licked her clit, she moaned. He sucked on her small, intensely sensitive button as Shane stroked her breast with one hand, his hot cock still pushing against her back.

"I think she likes that," Shane said

"Maybe she's too weak to fight us," Kyle said, then continued with his attentions.

Summer made a weak attempt to struggle, but Kyle's lips and tongue were driving her wild. Heat washed through her and she gasped, then wailed in release.

"She did like that. Maybe she'll be amenable to returning the favor," Shane suggested.

Kyle released her legs, and Shane lowered her until her feet touched the ground.

"She doesn't really have any choice," Kyle answered.

As Shane cupped her breasts, she felt the tension release on the rope holding her arms upright. Shane pressed down on her shoulders until she knelt on the ground, her arms still stretched above her head. The rope pulled taut again.

Something brushed against her mouth.

"Open up, honey," Kyle said.

She opened her mouth as he glided his cock between her lips.

"If you do a good job, we'll untie you."

She sucked on his cock, then swirled her tongue along the shaft. After a few moments, he pulled out.

"My turn," Shane said.

His cock pushed into her mouth, and she licked and sucked him.

They shifted back and forth, pushing first one cock, then the other into her mouth. She loved it. Each one was unique. Kyle's thick shaft with the bulbous head. Shane's more slender but longer member.

"Oh, yeah, honey. That's so good." Kyle's hand cupped around her head. He pushed in and out and she squeezed his thrusting cock inside her mouth. He groaned and stiffened. She knew he was going to . . . He erupted into her mouth.

He drew his cock free, and Shane's cock slid in. He pulsed in and out in short thrusts, and she swirled her tongue around his cock head. He drove deeper, bumping the back of her throat, then pulled back and pulsed again. She squeezed and sucked hard. Her mouth filled with hot liquid.

Kyle lifted her to her feet and pulled the blindfold from her eyes.

"I have an idea." Shane grabbed a wooden bench from the wall of the barn and stacked a wooden box on top of it. He then took a saddle from one of several at the side of the barn and propped it over the box.

A moment later, Summer found herself bent over the saddle. Shane coiled a rope around her ankles. After tugging her legs open wide, he tied her to the bench. The leather of the saddle cradled her pelvis and belly.

"You said you'd untie me." Not that she was unhappy with the current situation—in fact, she found it quite arousing—but her role demanded she ask the question.

"We will," Shane assured. "Later."

"Look what I found."

Summer lifted her head to see a naked Kyle step into her line of sight with a large, old mirror—cracked but still usable—and prop it against the wall in front of her. It gave

Summer a great view of herself, tied and bent over a saddle. Kyle walked around behind her and positioned his feet between hers, and she felt his hot cock press against her wet slit.

"No. You can't do this," she cried with mock desperation in her voice.

"Oh, baby. Yes, I can."

He lurched forward and slid into her, deep and hard. She gasped at his invasion. He thrust several times, caressing her insides with his hot, hard length as she watched in the mirror.

"No. Please stop." She sucked in air, feeling dizzy at the incredible pleasure of his cock filling her.

"Hey, partner. My turn," Shane said.

Kyle pulled free, and Shane stepped behind her. His cock pushed against her and drove inside.

"Ohhhh. No."

"Honey, you love my hard cock inside you." His fingers flicked over her clit, and she wailed.

"Oh, please," she cried, loving every stroke.

He thrust deeper, then pulled out and thrust again. She could see Kyle behind Shane, his gaze shifting back and forth from Kyle's cock penetrating her to the image in the mirror as he stroked his hard shaft.

She arched over the saddle, but that pulled her away from Shane's cock, so she pushed her backside upward to give him better access. His hands wrapped around her hips to hold her in place, and he pounded into her. Pleasure pummeled through her as his long, rigid cock glided in and out.

She gasped as a blissful swell of sensation surged through her.

Shane pulled his cock from her.

"Noooo," she wailed.

Kyle thrust into her.

She gasped. He was solid and thick. He thrust repeatedly. The pleasure that had slipped away with the loss of Shane built steadily again. She moaned.

Then he drew out.

She groaned.

"I think she's enjoying this too much," Kyle said.

Shane thrust into her, and she quivered in pleasure. Kyle stepped in front of her, holding his cock in his hand. She gazed up at him, then at his hard cock, and licked her lips. He stepped closer as Shane thrust deep into her. Kyle pressed his cock to her lips, and she opened. He pushed deep into her mouth.

Shane jerked into her again and again as she sucked on Kyle's big cock. Shane's finger swirled over her clit again, and she clamped tight around Kyle as pleasure shot through her. She sucked on his cock as she squeezed Shane's. Shane grunted and hot liquid erupted inside her. A spasm ran through her as intense pleasure shot through her entire body.

Kyle groaned, and his cock flooded her mouth. Shane continued to pump into her, and she moaned around Kyle's cock as an incredible orgasm pulsed through her. Kyle's cock slipped from her mouth as she wailed at the intensity of the incredible bliss.

She barely had time to catch her breath before the men unfastened the ropes, freeing her ankles and wrists, and Kyle threw her over his shoulder and carried her into the house. He raced up the stairs with Shane behind them.

"Don't think we're finished with you," Kyle said as he

entered the bedroom and thrust her onto the upholstered chair by the window.

She watched as Kyle grabbed a tube from the top of the dresser and opened it, then began stroking clear gel onto his hard cock. She licked her lips at the sight of his glistening member.

Shane tossed a pillow on the side of the bed, then grabbed her hand and pulled her from the chair. He eased her face first onto the bed, her stomach over the pillow so her legs draped over the side of the bed and her ass perched upward. Shane lay across the bed in front of her, his cock placed conveniently near her mouth. He wrapped his hand around his cock and pressed it to her lips. She sucked him inside. He stroked the hair from her face and cupped her cheek as Kyle's cock nudged against her ass.

She wiggled a little in a halfhearted attempt at showing a struggle. Kyle chuckled and clamped one hand around her hip to hold her still, then pushed forward. His cock head pushed hard against her small opening. The lubrication he'd applied allowed him to slip in fairly easily. He pushed forward slowly, until he filled her ass.

He then tucked one strong arm around her waist, and Shane's cock slipped from her mouth as Kyle tugged her back against him. He drew her up and led her backward toward the dresser. They were both standing now, Kyle leaning against the dresser for support, his cock still embedded in her ass.

She dropped her head back against his shoulder as Shane stood up and stepped in front of her. Kyle tucked his hands around her thighs and drew her legs upward, opening them. Shane stepped forward and his hard cock head brushed her opening. Anticipation swelled within her as she realized she was about to have two cocks—real cocks, not the plastic kind—inside her for the very first time.

Shane eased forward, pushing his long cock into her a little at a time. Kyle's cock twitched inside her ass as Shane's tunneled deeper inside her.

She was full. Front and back. Pressed between these two hard, male bodies. She nuzzled against Shane's neck, completely abandoning any pretense of resistance.

"You okay, sweetheart?" Shane murmured against her temple.

"Better than okay."

He drew back and eased forward. Her vagina swelled with his renewed invasion, sending delicious sensations tingling through her.

"Oh, that feels so good."

Kyle eased forward, pushing himself from the dresser. He drew back and eased forward. Her anal passage ached with the pleasurable stretching sensation. Shane's cock receded, then filled her again. The two men synchronized until they were both pushing into her and easing back at the same time.

"My God, that feels incredible."

Better than incredible!

Her breathing increased, her pulse rate skyrocketed. She could hear her heart thundering in her chest.

The men picked up speed, now surging into her with deeper thrusts. Blissful sensations surged through her . . . pulsing . . . quivering . . . Shane thrust hard and she gasped, then clung to him as ecstatic waves washed over her in an incredible, mind-numbing orgasm.

She wailed. Shane thrust a few more times and erupted inside her. Kyle groaned as he joined them with his own climax.

She rested her cheek against Shane's chest. She had never felt more cherished.

Sunshine shimmered from the hot black pavement as Max drove along the highway. Leaves on the tall trees sprinkled along the side of the highway quivered in the breeze, and purple wildflowers swayed in the meadows.

He knew the two men wouldn't have been comfortable with him hanging around outside, so he'd decided to go for a drive.

He tried not to think about Summer and the two men back in the barn. Tried not to imagine the two men kissing and touching her naked body while she hung helplessly from the ropes, finally enjoying what she'd longed to experience for so long. The men clearly cared about Summer, so not only would they plunge their cocks deep into her, they would touch her with tenderness and passion.

He should be pleased—Summer had grown immensely with his help, and now she'd achieved a major step forward. Not only had she finally started an intimate relationship with the two men she'd desired for years, but she was now taking part in a ménage à trois with them. She'd pushed past her boundaries and embraced her desires.

She really had blossomed since he'd met her . . . and he should be happy about that . . . but all he could think about were the two men kissing her, touching her, giving her immense pleasure. Two men she'd yearned for.

A fierce possessiveness launched through him . . . a nagging, intensely emotional side of him that wanted her all for himself. And that shocked him.

He didn't want entanglements with women. Short, torrid affairs suited him just fine. Being in control of when and where . . . and how long . . . suited him perfectly. The women he usually became involved with understood that. He would dominate . . . they would submit. Great sex, but no emotional attachments. And he prided himself on taking his partners to a deeper understanding of themselves. Then he'd move on. Everyone was happy.

But with Summer . . .

His fingers tightened around the steering wheel. Damn, he didn't like these feelings. He should leave. Now. Before this got any more complicated.

Fifteen

Summer stepped out of the shower and towel-dried her hair, then combed it out as she thought about the spectacular afternoon she'd experienced with Shane and Kyle. They had left half an hour ago, knowing Max would be returning to continue his weekend with her.

They hadn't seemed particularly pleased to leave her with another man, but she'd explained that this was the last time she'd see him, and she needed time to say good-bye.

After showering and dressing, she went back out to the barn. She had seen something out there that intrigued her.

She headed out the kitchen door and walked into the barn. There in the corner, partially covered by a tarp, she saw the wooden contraption with one hole on the right and a larger hole partially covered by the tarp. She lifted the tarp, revealing exactly what she'd hoped for. A stock. Two pieces of wood pressed together, forming three holes. The middle one was large enough to hold a neck, and the ones on each side were an appropriate size for wrists. Each opening was padded.

She pulled the tarp farther back and had to tug as it caught on something behind the stock. To her delight, she found it was more than just a stock on a stand. It was a sort of bench, like the whipping benches she'd seen in the dungeon at Sex-à-la-Gala. There was a place to rest her torso and two places for her knees. These, too, were padded.

She grinned. Next time she saw Tanya, she'd have to ask how this happened to wind up in her barn.

Summer tugged on the frame, hoping she'd be able to pull the device into the house, but it was a little too heavy and awkward to manage on her own. Determined, she examined it and found the stock could be removed from the bench, so she went in the house and grabbed a toolbox from the basement. Forty minutes later, she had the stock fully set up in the kitchen. She wiped it down with a damp cloth, removing the accumulated dust, then smiled at her handiwork.

Max had called about twenty minutes ago and told her he'd be there in half an hour. That meant she had ten minutes. She slipped into the bathroom and tugged off her clothes, then left them in a neat pile on the vanity. She checked her reflection in the mirror and brushed her hair to a glossy shine, then returned to the kitchen. The sight of the stock in the middle of the large country kitchen sent her heart thumping wildly. It looked so out of place. So wicked. And she felt wicked standing here, naked, in front of it.

She drew in a breath, then knelt down on the knee pads and pulled the attached leather straps around her calves, just behind her knees, and buckled them into place. She pulled up the top of the stock, and it creaked open. It had a spring mechanism and stayed up. Earlier, she'd placed a cord around the top of the stock so she could pull it closed. Now she grasped the cord loosely in her hand, rested her neck and wrists in the appropriate holes, then tugged on the cord. The top eased down and closed around her wrists and neck. Then the latch clicked closed. She pushed upward, but it didn't budge.

Her stomach clenched as she realized she had accidentally locked herself into this contraption, but she sucked in a deep breath to calm herself.

Excitement tingled through her. Max would be here soon.

She became extremely conscious of being locked up and totally vulnerable to anyone who might come in. With her knees on the pads and her head and arms in the stock, her behind was pushed up in the air, totally exposed. Her insides clenched with excitement. Anyone could walk in and take her.

"Well, what do we have here?"

Max! Behind her. She had positioned the stock so she'd see him come in from the living room, assuming he'd come in the front door, but he'd come in the door off the side of the kitchen. Now her naked back end was totally open to his view.

"My friends and I are very happy to see you."

Her face flushed. "Your . . ." She gulped. "Friends?"

Had he brought other people? Were Shane and Kyle with him? Or had he brought strangers?

He chuckled as he walked closer. His hand brushed over her bare derrière, then up her hip. He strolled around to face her. His hand stroked over the bulge in his pants, then down between his legs.

"Don't worry. Just these friends."

She sighed, but the sight of him stroking his growing bulge, and knowing how big his cock was, sent her hormones racing.

"Master, I have been very bad."

"Oh?" His eyebrows arched upward, and he strolled toward her. "And what has my bad girl done?"

"I've been with two other men and . . . I enjoyed it very much."

"Really? And what did these two men do to you?"

"They leaned me over a saddle and took me from behind."

He smiled. "Really?" He opened his zipper, then drew out his cock. She licked her lips at the sight of his long and very thick shaft. It was purple, and the veins seemed to pulse.

"Did you kiss the men with passion?"

"Yes."

"I want you to kiss me with passion, just as you did them."

Confused, she watched him step forward. Was he going to release her from the stock? So soon?

But he shifted his cock head toward her, and she realized what he wanted. She pressed her lips against his hard flesh as if it were a mouth, kissing it with passion. She slipped her tongue between her lips and teased the small opening on the tip. She moved her lips on him, her tongue stroking in circles. He eased forward a little, and she opened her mouth. His cock head sank into her. She pulsed around his hard shaft, licking the tip and stroking him with her whole mouth.

He drew back, then his lips captured hers for a moment before he stood up again.

"That was very nice, but I still need to punish you."

"Yes, Master." Anticipation trilled through her.

He moved behind her. His hands stroked over her buttocks, then she felt a sharp smack across her buttock. Her nipples blossomed into hard nubs. He stroked over her sore behind, soothing.

A sharp smack across her other buttock made her gasp. He stroked again.

He smacked several more times, leaving her breathless. Her vagina clenched, dripping shamelessly.

He stroked her buttocks again, round and round. As she waited for yet another slap, he slid a hand down her thigh and between her legs. He stroked her folds, and she could feel the slick liquid between her legs. Then his cock pushed against her and he thrust forward, impaling her in one stroke. She moaned, squeezing him inside her. He slid back.

A second later, she felt him push against her anus.

Oh, God, he's too big. The thought of his huge, broad cock gliding into her ass scared her.

She felt the pressure build as he pushed against her, then eased off. She sucked in a breath. When he pushed again, she had to say something.

"Master, it's too big."

The pressure eased.

He moved away, then walked past her and left the kitchen. Had she made him angry?

He returned a few moments later. He had a tube and a rolled-up towel in his hand. He walked past her.

"I'm putting lubricant on, Summer. It's one of those ones that warms up."

Summer had heard of them. When applied, they warmed to the touch.

She felt his cock press against her ass again, slick this time.

It pressed her opening wide as the tip pushed in a little.

"Oh, I—"

His hands stroked over her buttocks. "Summer, do you trust me?"

"I . . ."

His cock pushed a little more forward, and panic lanced through her, but she swallowed it back.

"It will be okay. Just trust me." He eased forward, then drew back again.

She sucked in air and tried to relax.

His cock eased forward and pushed in a little farther, stretching her wide.

Blind panic lanced through her. "No, it's too much."

He eased forward slowly. Her skin stretched around his cock head, and she knew it wasn't at its widest yet.

As he continued to ease forward, she gasped.

"No." She sucked in air. "Cat."

He stopped instantly. Slowly, he eased back.

She felt like crap. She wanted to trust him. She *did* trust him.

"Wait, Master. Don't stop. I do trust you."

"Summer, call me Max."

"I trust you, Max."

"I'm glad to hear that."

He pushed forward with a steady pressure, and she pushed back against him, pushing her internal muscles to open her as much as possible. Suddenly, he was in. His whole cock head immersed inside her. He continued to ease forward, filling her.

That couldn't be it. It didn't feel big enough.

Then she felt a cock press against her vagina.

"Oh," she cried. "Is someone else there?"

But there couldn't be. The way the big cock was penetrating her, there couldn't be two men behind her.

As it pushed inside, she realized the cock sliding into her vagina was Max's.

"No one else is here, Summer. I just have a very realistic cock made of a soft silicone. The lubricant warmed it up."

He continued to push forward until he was totally immersed. Oh, God, it felt wonderful being so full. With Max's cock.

He wrapped his arms possessively around her waist and kissed her back.

"Thank you for trusting me."

Then he began to move. He pushed both cocks into her, then drew them out, then into her again. Despite the variations she'd experienced this afternoon, she had never felt this full before. Max's huge cock filled her like no other man's could, and the extra cock stretching her ass . . . it was the most exquisite sensation.

As he moved within her, she felt an ecstatic release of pure pleasure, then her whole body began to tremble as her nerve endings sparked with delightful, mind-blowing bliss. It quivered through her entire body as waves of ecstasy pulsed through her, carrying her to heaven in an electrifying release.

Max pumped deep and hot liquid filled her, sending her over the edge again. She wailed, arching her back, his hand pressed firmly against her stomach.

He nuzzled her back, kissing the base of her neck, and stroked along her spine.

"You are beautiful." His words warmed her.

His huge cock glided along her passage as he drew back, then he gently removed the dildo. Even though he wasn't even out yet, she missed his cock already.

As Max pulled out of her hot, moist passage, he tamped down the disturbing emotions fluttering through him. He'd asked her to trust him . . . and she had. The extreme sense of satisfaction that gave him unnerved him. Of course, he wanted her to trust him, but it shouldn't mean so much to him. And he had been totally shocked at his need for her to say his name. Not Master, which usually turned him on immensely . . . and still did. But he'd needed her to connect with him as a person, not as a Dom.

And he still wanted that.

"Would you like to be freed?"

She stared at the floor. "Whatever is your pleasure, Master."

A deep need shot through him, and he had to clamp down on his senses in order to move slowly and deliberately. He leaned down and unbuckled the leather straps from around her calves, then stepped toward the stock and released the latch. He lifted the top and helped her stand up. Her muscles would be stiff. Once she stood up, he drew her into his arms and captured her mouth, his lips moving on hers in a gentle caress, his tongue stroking her inner lips delicately, but as his control edged away, need pulsed through him and he took her lips with a blazing passion. Finally, he scooped her up and carried her up the stairs to the bedroom. He tossed her onto the bed and climbed over her.

"Summer, I want you. More than I've wanted any other woman before."

He pressed his cock to her slit, needing to possess her immediately. He thrust into her.

She gasped. "Oh, Master."

He lifted his head from nuzzling her neck and stared deep into her eyes.

"Call me Max."

Her eyes widened at the need sparking in his eyes.

"Max," she murmured.

At the sound of his name, he thrust deep.

"Say it again."

"Max." She moaned as he thrust and thrust again.

Sparks flared between them. Pleasure drummed through them both. He could tell she was close. He thrust again, and she started to moan.

"Am I making you come, Summer?"

"Yes." She wailed.

"Tell me."

"You're making me . . . ah . . . come."

"Say my name."

"You're making me come, Max. Oh . . ." She clung to him. "I'm coming. Oh, Max."

At the sound of his name on her lips as she swept into orgasm, Max exploded within her, holding her body tightly to his.

As she relaxed on the bed, then fell asleep in his arms, Max struggled with what had just happened. It had been incredible. He had come more intensely than he ever had before. Hearing his name on her lips as she'd reached the pinnacle of ecstasy had affected him more than he thought possible.

And that disturbed him.

Sixteen

Max watched as sunlight flickered across Summer's eyes and she opened her eyelids. He gazed at her, a big smile on his face. A soft breeze sent tendrils of her long auburn hair across her cheek—the same one that fluttered through the leaves outside, sending dappled sunlight into the bedroom window and across her face.

"Good morning, sleepyhead," he said.

"Morning." She cleared her throat at the sound of her sleep-raspy voice.

She rolled against him, and her soft lips nibbled at his raspy chin. The feel of her soft body against him . . . the delicate floral scent of her . . . filled him with joy. He wrapped his arms around her and pulled her on top of him, then kissed her tenderly.

She pushed herself up, grinning down at him as she straddled him, her pussy hot against his stomach.

"So the big strong Dom will allow a mere female to sit on top of him?"

"Only you."

But he wrapped his hands around her waist and lifted

her sideways, then snuggled her against his body. If she kept sitting on him like that, he'd be inside her before either of them knew what happened.

She laughed, then nuzzled his cheek.

"So do you have a lot of . . . uh . . . women who . . . ?"

"Subs?"

She nodded. The inquisitive look in her eyes told him it was more than idle curiosity.

"I only have one at a time." He kissed her nose. "And right now, that's you."

She smiled. "I see.

Summer liked the idea that she was the only woman in Max's life right now. Which was totally crazy because he was one of three men in her life right now, and he knew it. In fact, he encouraged it.

She traced circles across his broad chest, enjoying the feel of his hard muscles under her fingertip.

"How did you become a Dom? I mean . . . is it something you've always been or something you decided you liked, or . . . ?" She shrugged, not really sure what she was asking but curious how someone threw himself into such a role so thoroughly.

He tucked his hands behind his head and stared at the ceiling.

"No, I didn't use to live the lifestyle. To tell you the truth, my wife and I used to enjoy absolutely vanilla sex."

Wife? Oh, God . . . was he . . . married? No, he wouldn't . . .

"Stop looking so panicked. I'm not married. I'm a widower."

Her heart compressed. She pushed herself up on her elbow and stared down at him.

"Oh, Max. I'm so sorry."

He nodded. "My wife died five years ago. It was tough. I had a hard time getting past it. Afterward, I guess I just wanted . . . something completely different."

Her heart ached at the thought of Max in misery after losing someone he loved . . . and she was a little jealous that he had loved someone else . . . which was insane . . . and totally selfish on her part.

She couldn't think of anything to say, so she just kissed him. Gently. Tenderly. Then wrapped her arms around him and held him close.

Max's chest tightened at the feel of Summer holding him in a loving embrace. His heart felt as though it might explode at the tenderness. Powerful emotions welled inside him. Emotions he hadn't dealt with in years. The pain of losing Elena was strong, but it was overshadowed by the desire to be wanted and loved by one special woman. To be held by someone who considered him the most important person in her life. To be truly loved by someone.

Finally, he couldn't stand the closeness any longer. He gently eased himself from Summer's embrace and sat up.

"I think it's time for breakfast."

She sat up and stretched her arms. "Sounds like a great idea."

He raised an eyebrow.

"Oh, you want me to make it?" she asked.

He continued to stare at her expectantly.

"Master?" she added quickly.

"Make me an omelet with onions, peppers, cheese, and . . ." He paused at her pursed lips. "Is there a problem?"

"I don't know how to make omelets. Well, I know how, but trust me, you won't want to eat one I make."

He chuckled. "Fine. I'll direct you." At her dubious stare, he added, "You'll slice and dice, et cetera, but I'll cook the omelet." He leaned down and kissed her, enjoying the delicate play of her sweet lips on his, then grinned. "I'll meet you in the shower in ten minutes."

She rolled from the bed and ambled across the room to the bathroom. Ten minutes later, Max stepped into the bathroom to the sound of the shower running. Summer stood by the shower door, totally naked.

She pushed open the glass door as he approached. "I hope the temperature of the water is to your liking, Master."

He grinned and tugged her into the large tiled shower, then leaned her against the wall farthest from the spray of warm water. She let out a small gasp, probably at the cold tiles against her back. He pinned her to the wall with his warm body and held her hands at each side of her head, then took her lips with passion. His cock tightened at the feel of her soft breasts pressed against his chest.

Summer felt Max's cock grow rigid against her and wondered when he would thrust it inside her, but he released her and stepped back into the spray. The water ran over his shoulders and flowed in rivulets down his sculpted pectoral muscles, over his tight, well-defined abdominals, then trickled down his hard-muscled thighs.

Her gaze flickered to the round sacs below the sprinkling of dark curls at his pelvis, then followed his long, thick shaft upward to the bulbous head. She drew the tip of her tongue around her lips, imagining it gliding around the ridge of his cock head.

He smiled and handed her a bar of soap. "Here, Summer. I want you to wash your breasts."

She ran the bar of soap over one breast, then the other, then stroked over the mounds of flesh until they were slick and foamy with soap.

"Now, between your legs."

She rubbed the bar of soap between her hands, then placed it in the soap dish mounted to the wall. She stroked her sudsy hands down her belly, then over her folds of flesh. Around and down, over the slick, tender flesh. Heat rose in her.

His gaze followed her movements intently. "Don't forget your clit. We want that nice and clean."

She stroked over her clit and moaned a little at the delicious sensation.

"Inside your pussy, too."

She continued stroking her clit with one hand, then slid the fingers of her other hand inside and swirled around. His hands covered her breasts, and his caresses, combined with the heat inside her, made her desperate for more.

She shifted her hand from her clit to wrap around his thick shaft.

He leaned in to whisper in her ear, "Do you want me?"

"Yes, Master."

He chuckled. "Good."

He slid his hand down her belly, then over her clit, then drew her hand away and slid his long, masculine fingers inside her and stroked her inner walls.

Her eyelids fluttered closed, and she moaned.

"Is it a deep yearning you can barely control?"

She nodded.

"I can't hear you."

"Yes . . . Master. Yes."

"A yearning for what?"

"For you to touch me. For you to push your big cock into me and . . . make me come."

As he stroked inside her, his thumb flicked over her clit, and she gasped.

"You want me to make you come?"

"Yes, please, Master."

He stepped back, his hands leaving her body . . . so needy and frustrated. She groaned.

"That is a yearning I want to make last. For a very long time." He smiled at her. "Now wash me."

She ran the bar of soap over his hard, muscled chest, then over his taut belly. She cupped his firm buttocks as she ran her soapy hands around and around. She grabbed the bar of soap again and rubbed it until her hands were covered in suds, then she ran them under his balls and soaped them good, then stroked up his cock. She wrapped both hands around his shaft and stroked up and down, hoping she was causing him the same level of tormented desire he'd built in her. His rock-hard cock twitched in her hands . . . a good sign.

When they stepped from the shower, she picked up a white, fluffy towel and patted his body lovingly, ensuring she dried every inch of him. He dried her with the same attention to detail.

In the bedroom, when she reached for her stack of clothing, he planted his hand on top of them.

"No clothes."

187

Max put down his book and gazed at Summer, sitting quietly in the chair beside him. Her long, silky auburn hair flowed over her shoulders and curled around her full breasts. Her dusky rose aureoles pebbled at his inspection, the nipples peaking forward. His gaze slid down to her pussy and the dark auburn curls waxed into a neat triangle.

He smiled. "I have something for you."

She gazed at him, a half smile on her lips. He picked up the flat black box from the coffee table.

"Come over here and kneel in front of me."

As she obeyed, he pulled off the lid, then drew out the black leather collar.

"Hold up your hair."

She scooped up her auburn waves and held them while he fastened the collar around her neck.

"Now go and sit in the easy chair," he said.

After breakfast, he had instructed her to slide a dildo inside her back opening—one with a flat end that would stop it from sliding all the way inside and would allow her to sit comfortably. As she crossed the room, he could see the flat purple end between her cheeks, the only part of it visible. She sat down, her fingers toying with the one-inch metal ring on the front of the collar. He picked up a slender gold bell with an ornate handle.

"When I ring this once, I want you to caress your breasts. When I ring it twice, caress your pussy. Don't touch yourself unless I tell you, or ring the bell. And don't come until I give you permission."

"Yes, Master."

He loved hearing her call him Master. With a deep

sense of satisfaction, he settled back and picked up his book, though he couldn't read a word. Not with the knowledge of Summer sitting across the room naked and collared, with a cock inside her ass. After about five minutes, he picked up the bell and rang it once. She stroked her breasts, then her fingers teased the nipples. Soon she began to pinch them. He rang the bell twice, and her hands glided down her belly to slip between her legs.

Sunlight glistened from her fingers as they slipped in and out of her slit. His cock throbbed at the sight. He rang the bell again, once, and her hands returned to her breasts. The nipples jutted out, hard and needy. He rang once again, and she glanced at him questioningly.

"If I repeat the same number of rings, it means stop."

Her hands fell to the armrests. He picked up his book again and pretended to read as his cock twitched and strained in longing. Barely ten minutes went by before he picked up the bell again and rang it once. He watched as her hands toyed with her nipples, while the tip of her tongue traced her lips. He rang twice and watched her hands glide downward with intense anticipation. As her fingers slid into her slit, his heart thundered in his chest. Her fingers stroked over her clit, then drove into her slit again. She worked them back and forth, then deep into her pussy.

Her head fell back and she moaned.

"Oh, Master. Please, may I come?"

Immediately, he rang the bell twice. She hesitated, then rather than stopping immediately, she swirled her fingers around inside her before finally pulling out.

"You have been disobedient. Kneel down on the floor."

She pushed herself from the chair and knelt in front of

it. He stood up and opened the drawer in the table beside the couch, then pulled out a special gag he'd placed there in anticipation of just such a punishment. A short rubber cock attached to a black strap. He stepped toward her.

"Open your mouth."

Obediently, she opened her mouth wide. He longed to slide his cock into her mouth, to feel her hot mouth embrace it and draw it deep into her, but he held his yearning in check. He placed the short cock of the gag into her mouth, then buckled the black leather strap behind her head.

"Glide your tongue around the cock. Imagine it's my cock."

This would keep her thinking about having his cock in her mouth.

"Now go into the kitchen. You'll find a wooden stool under the desk in the corner. Bring it back here."

As she walked into the kitchen, he returned to the drawer and pulled out the rope. She returned a moment later with the stool.

"Put it here." He indicated a spot about two feet from the couch—within easy reach. She set it down.

"Now turn around."

He drew her hands together behind her back, coiled the rope around her wrists, and tied it snugly.

"Sit on the stool."

She sat down. He settled back on the couch and picked up his book again. He forced himself to read a few pages, though none of the words actually made it to his brain, then stood up and approached her. He fiddled with the black metal snaps on the front of the gag and pulled out the short cock. The ring inside the gag kept her mouth wide open in an O shape. He stepped toward her, anticipation sending his pulse soaring.

With eager anticipation, Summer watched Max's big cock approach her face. She sucked in a deep breath, more than ready for him. He pushed his cock head to her lips, then eased forward. It pressed through the ring and into her mouth. Her tongue darted forward, and she licked the tip of him as he eased forward. His cock head filled her mouth, and she swirled her tongue around him. He pushed deeper, his shaft gliding along the ring into her mouth. She lapped at the underside of his shaft, then dragged her tongue along him as he drew back. He thrust forward and back in short strokes as she licked and squeezed. She swirled her tongue around and around, then tunneled into the underside of the corona. He stopped thrusting and allowed her to swirl and lick the very sensitive ridge. His cock pulsed inside her. He was going to come.

He groaned, then pulled his hard cock from her mouth. He hooked his finger through the ring on her collar and tugged. She felt herself pulled to her feet, then tugged toward the couch. He released her and sat down, then positioned her, still standing, between his knees. He cupped her breasts, then leaned forward and sucked one hard nipple into his hot mouth. He shifted to the other and sucked hard, making her gasp.

His hand grasped the back of her head, and she bent over as he drew her face closer, then pressed his tongue to her mouth, still held wide open by the ring of the gag. Her tongue danced with his for a moment, then he released her and slid his hands between her legs, then slid two long fingers into her damp passage. He stroked the inner walls, while his other hand found the flat end of the cock in her back passage and he moved it in a small circle, sending intense pleasure careening through her. She gasped for air.

"Do you want to come?"

She nodded emphatically. His hand slid from inside her, and he grasped his cock.

"Then climb up here."

She moved forward, resting her knees on either side of his, anticipation thrumming through her. He held her waist, helping her balance since her hands were still bound behind her back. He positioned his cock head against her slit and she lowered herself down, tears forming in her eyes at the intense pleasure of his cock driving into her and stretching her passage wide. With the cock in her ass, she felt extremely full and aching for an orgasm.

She tried to lift herself up so she could feel his penis glide within her, but he held her hips tightly, keeping her pinned to his body.

"Stay put for a second and I'll take off the gag."

She nodded, and he reached behind her head and unfastened the straps. Her stretched jaw muscles relaxed as he removed the ring from her mouth. He captured her lips and kissed her, his mouth moving on hers. She thrust her tongue into his mouth, and he met hers with lustful exuberance. He cradled her head in his big hands and drove his tongue into her mouth, then thrust several times. When he finally released her, she gasped for air.

"Now, you said you want to come."

"Yes, Master." The words came out deep and husky.

"All right. You can have three strokes. No more."

She almost uttered a protest but caught herself in time. "Yes, Master."

She drew herself up and thrust down on him. His cock drove deep into her, and pleasure rocketed through her. She squeezed him as she drew up and drove down again. Her pleasure peaked, but not enough. She repeated the action and on her downward thrust squeezed him tightly. Intense pleasure gripped her, but now she rested against him, intensely stimulated but with no orgasm in sight.

His long, hard cock filled her deeply and stretched her wide. She squeezed him and pivoted her pelvis forward to press more tightly against him, giving her clit more stimulation. If only she could slip her hand down there to flick her clit, but her hands were still bound behind her. She squeezed his hard shaft, then released, squeezed, then released. She felt her pleasure surge. She shifted forward as she squeezed, then back, but never stroking upward since he had forbidden that. She found a motion that caused her pleasure to spiral upward. She sucked in air, faster and faster as she squeezed and shifted. She pulled on him, then released. As she felt her pulse increasing, his finger found her clit and he tweaked. Waves of pleasure pulsed through her.

"Are you close, baby?"

"Yes, I think so. . . ." She squeezed again, and he jerked upward a little.

That did it. She moaned, then things started to go gray. He thrust upward, and pleasure spun through her in dizzying intensity. He grabbed her waist and lifted her and brought her back down, then lifted again. She wailed as the climax erupted through her. He rolled her beneath him and thrust into her . . . again and again. His cock filled her . . .

deep and hard. Again and again . . . as she wailed in release. Pounding harder and harder until she filled with infinite bliss . . . and the universe slipped away.

Blackness surrounded her.

"Summer . . ."

She sucked in air as she became aware of her surroundings. She'd lost consciousness.

"My God, Summer! You are so fucking sexy."

He unfastened the ropes around her wrists and pulled her into his arms. His chest hairs tickled her nose as he held her tight and secure to his body.

Once they'd both caught their breath, he scooped her up and carried her to the bedroom, where he caressed her all over, then thrust into her in another spectacular lovemaking session. He couldn't seem to keep his hands off her for the next several hours, then he held her all night long. She felt warm and protected in his arms. Even loved.

Damn it. She could get used to this.

Shane scanned the report the front desk clerk had just handed him, checking the vacation requests from the security staff for the next month. He signed the approval on the bottom of the page and handed it back. He caught sight of Summer heading across the lobby toward her shop. His jaw clenched at the half smile curling her lips. He could almost feel the sex simmering from her.

Kyle strode to the desk and handed over a large envelope— probably the signed paychecks for the staff—then glanced toward Shane. He quirked an eyebrow as the shop door closed behind Summer.

"I noticed her arrive in the parking lot a few minutes ago with Delaney," Kyle said.

Both he and Kyle knew exactly where she'd been. His stomach clenched at the thought she'd been in the arms of another man.

Sure, he knew she'd been away with the guy for the weekend, which Shane hated, but he'd assumed Sunday night would be the end of it. The fact that Delaney had dropped her off this morning . . . did that mean he'd be hanging around for a while?

Summer had made it clear she wanted a relationship with Shane. And Kyle, too. But Shane could handle sharing her with his best friend . . . especially after that stupendous afternoon at Tanya's country house. What he couldn't handle was her continuing a relationship with Max Delaney at the same time . . . despite the fact the guy had helped them get it together on Saturday. The three of them would have worked it out eventually. Shane didn't need Max Delaney's help. Nor did he like the idea of Max treating Summer like some kind of slave.

Shane glanced at Kyle to gauge his reaction, but Kyle simply picked up a pile of folders the desk clerk handed him, then headed toward his office. Shane watched Kyle disappear down the hallway off the lobby, surprised at his calmness. Shane, on the other hand, gritted his teeth and decided to get to the bottom of things.

Seventeen

Summer opened her desk drawer and dropped her purse inside, then started her computer. Max was returning to New York today. Their time together was at an end—as it should be, since it was only meant to be a weekend fling. They'd had some fun, and Max had helped her move forward with her life. Now it was time to move on. The fact that she now longed for more than that was *her* problem.

At a tapping on her open door, she glanced up. Shane stood inside the doorway, looking tall, handsome, and . . . concerned.

Last night, lying in Max's arms had been . . . heaven, but she needed to get back to reality. And seeing Shane standing there—his broad shoulders and muscular arms filling out his blue shirt so very nicely, his narrow waist accentuating his broad chest, and his familiar blue eyes matching the vivid blue of the cloudless sky outside her window—she realized reality was a pretty spectacular place.

Memories of Saturday afternoon—Shane holding her close, his solid body pressed against hers, his cock gliding into her, while Kyle matched him stroke for stroke—quivered through her, leaving her breathless.

"Good morning." She smiled. "It's a little early for coffee break."

"I know. May I come in?"

"Of course."

He stepped inside and closed the door behind him. He didn't return her smile as he sat in her guest chair and folded his hands between his knees.

"Summer, what exactly is going on with us?"

"Us?" She fiddled with a pen on her desk. "You know that I care about Kyle, too, and—"

"I don't mean that. I know we have to figure out the three of us, but . . . are you still seeing this other guy?"

Guilt washed through her as she realized she'd been selfish going off with Max. But Max had helped her come to terms with her issues about starting a relationship with Shane and Kyle. Without Max's help, the three of them would still be pretending to be just friends.

"Max just showed up on Friday and . . ." Thoughts stammered through her head. She was sure Shane didn't really want to know the specifics about her and Max. He wanted to know that Max wasn't a threat.

She stood up. "Shane, I really want to continue what you, Kyle, and I have started. Max just wanted one last weekend with me, and now I'll probably never see him again."

"Probably?"

Damn, that was a slip of the tongue . . . based on wishful thinking.

"We had a fling, but it's over now. I'm ready to figure

things out with you and Kyle. And if this whole thing is too much for you, I completely understand. I never expected—"

"You're attracted to this guy because he ties you up, right?"

Her gaze bounced to his, then away again. She picked up a pen and fiddled with it.

"There is something exciting about being dominated and—"

"I get it," he growled, not wanting to hear the gory details. "You like someone who takes charge. An authority figure."

He stood up, towering over her, and tugged his wallet out of his pocket, then flashed his security badge.

"Ma'am, I'm afraid you're under arrest."

Eighteen

Before Summer knew what was happening, Shane produced a pair of handcuffs and flicked a cold metal cuff around one of her wrists, then the other. The hard steel against her skin sent excitement skittering through her.

"Stand up and turn around."

Her eyes widened, but she obeyed. With his hands around her waist, he guided her to face the desk.

"Lean forward. Rest your hands on the desk."

The chain clanked on the wood as she flattened her hands on the desk and leaned forward, as instructed.

"I'm going to have to search you, ma'am."

Anticipation quivered through her as he grasped her shoulders, then slid his hands down her arms. When he slipped those strong hands under her arms, then glided forward over her breasts, she felt faint from the intense arousal shuddering through her.

He cupped her breasts and pressed them together, then stroked over them, his fingers and thumbs squeezing firmly. Her nipples puckered and she wanted him to strip off her clothes and touch her naked skin. Suck on her nipples.

As though reading her thoughts, he grabbed the sides of her blouse and tore it open. She gasped as several buttons went flying.

He tugged down on the lacy cups of her bra and tucked them under her breasts, then stroked over her naked mounds of flesh with his big hands. Cupping them . . . squeezing them . . . until she moaned.

He continued gliding his hands downward . . . over her ribs . . . around her hips . . . down her legs to her ankles.

"Open your legs, ma'am."

Oh, God, yes.

She widened her stance, her insides melting with need. He glided one hand up her inner thigh and under her skirt, while the other circled over one buttock, then the other . . . round and round, driving her crazy with need. . . . He cupped her mound, only the thin fabric of her panties between him and her naked skin.

He drew the crotch of her panties to one side and slid a finger inside her, then another. Heat pulsed through her, and she clenched around him. He stroked. Slowly. Thoroughly.

Then he withdrew and turned her around to face him. He grasped her wrist and fiddled. The cuff opened, and in a quick, sure movement, he drew one of her arms behind her, then the other, and she felt the cuff grip her wrist again, this time behind her back.

His gaze slid down her body and back up again, resting on her naked breasts. Her blouse hung loosely at her sides. A devilish grin turned up his lips, then disappeared as he put on the authoritative expression again.

"Ma'am, since I haven't found anything, I might be convinced to let you go. As long as you intend to be . . . cooperative."

She nodded, her heart thumping. She intended to be stunningly cooperative!

He unzipped his fly and reached inside, then drew out his quite erect cock. Long with a thick shaft, the cock head more subdued than Kyle's. He leaned against the desk, holding his cock pointed toward her.

"Sit down."

She obeyed, sinking into her office chair. He grabbed the armrests and rolled her toward him.

His cock stared at her, waiting. She leaned forward and licked the tip of him, then she wrapped her lips around him and glided downward. She longed to wrap her hands around his hot, hard cock . . . to stroke up and down. But they were cuffed behind her. She drew back, keeping only his cock head in her mouth while she twirled her tongue around and around the tip. She glided forward again and sucked. He groaned.

She bobbed up and down, sucking and licking him, feeling him twitch in her mouth.

"Whoa there." He pulled his cock from her mouth, then drew her to her feet. "I don't want to finish this just yet."

He grabbed a small striped cushion from the easy chair she had in the corner and set it on the desktop, then pushed aside her laptop, papers, and pens.

"Ma'am, put your head on the desk."

She stood up, then leaned forward and rested her forehead on the pillow. Shane stroked her ass, then down her thighs. He eased forward, his thighs pressing her legs open. His cock head nestled against her wet slit. He thrust forward, impaling her with one sure stroke. She moaned. The feel of his cock embedded inside her, twitching in anticipation, and the metal cuffs biting into her wrists, combined to send her catapulting to the edge.

Shane drew back and thrust forward again, and her breath caught. He thrust in and out. Pleasure built within her, climbing with each penetrating thrust. His fingers found her clit, and he toyed with it as his cock plowed into her. Deeper. Faster.

A frenzy of sensation careened through her like a cloud of butterflies fluttering across her nerve endings. Heat exploded through her, and she wailed in sheer bliss. Shane ground deep into her and groaned his release.

Kyle returned to his office to find the door closed. Shane had called him to the lobby for something supposedly urgent, then when Kyle arrived there, the concierge told him that Shane had left a message that he'd see him later.

Kyle opened the door and stepped into his office. Shane stood grinning at him.

"What was that all about?" Kyle dropped the mail, which he'd picked up at the front office, on his desk.

"I needed your approval on something."

"Yeah, what's that?"

"Close the door first," Shane said.

Kyle closed the door, then Shane swiveled Kyle's big leather desk chair, which had been facing away from him, and for the first time, Kyle realized Summer sat in the chair. Wearing handcuffs.

"What's going on?"

Her top was also missing a number of buttons, and it

draped open, revealing her naked breasts spilling over her bra.

"Captain, I arrested this woman, but I think we might want to be lenient with her. I came for your permission to release her."

Kyle smiled. "Lenient? I don't think so."

He locked the door, then walked toward Summer, grabbed the chain between the cuffs, and pulled her to her feet. He leaned her back against the desk until she was perched on the edge, then he lifted her knee and set her foot on the chair. When he pushed back her skirt, he was delighted to see her pussy was naked.

"Officer Curtis, sit down."

Shane raised an eyebrow but sat in the chair, staring at Summer's pussy, too.

"I think she should be punished. I would like to hear the prisoner scream."

Shane leaned forward and pressed his mouth to her pussy. The sight made Kyle's cock raging hard. He unzipped and brought it out. Summer sucked in air as Shane's head shifted on her opening, then she moaned. Kyle stepped close to the desk, presenting his cock to her.

"Open your mouth."

She immediately leaned down and opened her mouth, and he glided inside. She reached for him with her bound hands and wrapped her fingers around his shaft as she sucked his cock. Her hot moisture had his member pulsing. He sank deeper into her mouth, then glided back and forth several times. Shane licked her clit as his hand reached up and stroked over her breast.

Pleasure pulsed through Kyle, and he tugged his cock

from her mouth before it was too late. She moaned as Shane's head bobbed up and down between her legs. Her chained hands clutched at Shane's hair, then she flung her head back and wailed.

She looked absolutely angelic when she came.

As soon as Shane moved back, Kyle stepped around the desk and grasped both her legs, then pressed her thighs wide apart. He pressed his cock to her slick opening and thrust inside.

She was hot. Wet. And tight, as her muscles clamped around him. He drew back and drove into her. She moaned. He thrust in a steady rhythm, watching her lovely face as she gasped and moaned in pleasure. He increased his pace, plunging deeper and faster.

"Yes, oh, yes." She gasped, then wailed as her body quivered with spasms.

He groaned as his body tensed, then his cock exploded inside her. He rocked his pelvis several more times, extending her pleasure. Finally her moans subsided, and he drew her close to his body and held her. She sighed in his arms.

He withdrew from her body, then he kissed her, showing her with his gentle passion how much he loved being with her.

His heart skipped a beat.

Damn it, he was in love with her. And he'd take odds Shane was in love with her, too. That alone would be complicated enough, but with this other guy . . .

He smiled at her, and she smiled back, her eyes aglow.

"So why were we playing the policemen and the prisoner?"

"Shane thought he should arrest me for seeing another

guy. I hope that my behavior during my incarceration has proven to both of you how much you guys mean to me and that he is not a threat."

Kyle nodded. He had no doubt she believed Delaney was not a threat, but Kyle wasn't so sure. Even though the guy had left this morning, Kyle had little doubt they'd be seeing him again.

Summer pulled open the door and smiled at Kyle and Shane standing on her doorstep, Kyle carrying two bags of groceries and Shane with a bottle of wine and a case of beer.

She closed the door behind her, then felt herself spun around and pulled into Shane's arms. His lips captured hers, and his playfully teasing tongue stirred her. She stroked her fingers through his blond, wavy hair. His tall, muscular body pressed against hers made her feel soft and feminine. He released her lips and smiled down at her.

"Hi, sweetheart."

Kyle returned from the kitchen and drew her from Shane's arms into his own.

"My turn."

Kyle's lips claimed hers as if he wanted to show his possession of her. Not from Shane, but from Max. Ever since the weekend, every time they were together like this, she felt he was competing . . . to show her he . . . they . . . were better for her than Max.

His tongue dove into her mouth and stroked until she responded in kind. Her heart pounded in her chest, and her breathing increased.

Shane chuckled as he picked up the wine and beer he'd abandoned on the foyer floor.

"Geez, man. Let her up for air."

Kyle's mouth released her, but his intent gaze did not. He took her hand and led her into the kitchen.

Shane began unpacking the brown paper grocery bags on the counter. He tossed three packages wrapped in butcher's paper on the counter.

"We brought steaks," Shane said.

She leaned toward the counter to read the scrawl on the labels. "T-bones. They look big."

Shane grabbed her around the waist and pulled her against him, then kissed her lightly. "Sure. We need to keep up our strength to satisfy our lovely lady." He grinned. "And you . . . well, you have to keep up your energy, because after we finish those steaks, our appetites will be piqued for"—he nipped her ear—"dessert."

As Shane's lips captured hers again, she felt Kyle's hands encircle her waist.

"Hey, buddy. You've got to share the woman," Kyle said.

When Shane's lips released hers, he gave her a wink, then allowed Kyle to turn her around. Kyle captured her mouth again in a passionate melding of lips. Her heartbeat accelerated at their intense attention.

Shane opened the fridge door and placed several bottles of beer inside. He grabbed a couple of cold ones and twisted them open, then placed one on the counter near Kyle.

"Summer, you want a cooler?" Shane asked.

Kyle released her mouth, then stroked her cheek as he continued to gaze at her.

"Uh . . . yes, please." She eased away from Kyle and finished unpacking the brown paper bag sitting beside the steaks.

Shane grabbed a mixed berry vodka cooler from the fridge and twisted open the cap before handing it to her.

"So how does it feel having two men attending to your every need?" Shane asked. "You know, you really are living every woman's fantasy, right?"

She smiled. "I know."

If only this real-life fantasy-come-true weren't complicated by thoughts of yet another man . . . one who filled her with a longing to be tied up and tormented in a most exquisite way.

A man who was now out of her life.

Kyle took the steaks and unwrapped them, then put them on a plate.

"Kyle. Look alive." Shane tossed him a small spice bottle from the spice rack on the counter.

Kyle caught it in one hand, then Shane tossed him another. Summer's breath held as she saw a third bottle fly across the room—that spice rack and set of fancy spice bottles had been a gift from her mother—but Kyle tossed the first bottle in the air, caught the third, and then was juggling the three bottles in the air. Round and round.

Summer just watched, wide-eyed, while he tossed bottles in circles several times, then gently placed one on the counter, then two, then three . . . all intact.

She clapped. "Kyle, I didn't know you could juggle."

"I have a lot of talents you're not aware of," he said as he winked at her.

She remembered how he'd dominated her in his office—it had been such an incredible turn-on.

"I see."

207

Shane chuckled. "Don't listen to him. He's a one-trick pony."

Pony. Instantly, an image of pony-girl popped into her head, and she could imagine herself essentially naked, wearing only the leather harness, high-heeled shoes, and feather atop her head, then being ridden by both these stallions.

Kyle laughed good-naturedly as Shane took a knife and sliced a big onion. Kyle placed mushrooms and peppers beside the cutting board, ready to go.

"I'll go start the barbecue." Kyle headed out the patio door.

Summer folded up the paper bags, then opened the bagged lettuce and emptied it into a large salad bowl. Within ten minutes, they had everything ready to go. She followed Shane out the patio door onto the deck. Summer set the table, then settled on one of the patio chairs to enjoy the evening breeze.

Soon the aroma of steak filled the air as Shane flipped the meat with the long metal tongs.

"Dinner in five minutes," he announced.

Summer took a sip of her cooler as she glanced at the table to see if she'd forgotten anything. The steak sauce. She stood up and slid open the patio doors.

The phone was ringing inside the house. She stepped inside and headed toward the phone, but the answering machine picked up. She froze as she heard Max's voice.

Nineteen

"Summer, it's Max. I want to see you again. I'm coming back to Port Smith tomorrow evening. I'll call when I get in."

She snatched up the phone.

"Max, I thought last weekend was the last time we'd see each other."

"I know. That's what I'd intended. . . . I know you're still trying to figure things out with Kyle and Shane, but . : ."

Despite knowing this was a totally bad idea, that she should just tell him in a firm tone that things were over between them, she couldn't stop herself from asking, "But what, Max?"

"Damn, I wanted to do this in person, but . . . Summer, ever since I lost my wife, I closed myself off. I was afraid to lose someone I care for so deeply again. . . . But since I met you . . . you're all I can think about. . . . Summer, you've opened a part of me I thought was closed forever."

Summer sank against the kitchen counter, her heart aching and confusion swirling through her. Max had opened his heart to her. She couldn't say no to seeing him again. Not after that heartrending confession. But . . . what about Shane and Kyle?

"Summer?" Max's voice jarred her out of her daze.

"Yes. Of course. I'll see you tomorrow." She hung up, feeling numb. Warm male hands wrapped around her waist and drew her against a warm male body.

"That was him, wasn't it," Kyle said.

"Yes. He's coming into town tomorrow, and . . . I've agreed to see him."

After cleaning up the dinner dishes, they sat on her couch, Shane and Kyle on either side of her. No one said a word. The mood was thick with tension. Summer let out a sigh.

"Will you guys just talk to me about this? I know you're upset about Max—"

"Of course we're upset." Shane's blue eyes flared. "You told us it was over with him, now you're seeing him again."

Summer sighed. "I understand how you feel, and I'm sorry to be so horribly unfair to you." She folded her hands in her lap and stared at them. "Maybe I should work out my relationship with Max before the three of us take things any further."

Kyle's strong fingers wrapped around her hand, and he stroked her palm.

"Here's what I think." His gaze captured hers. "I don't want you to be in a relationship with us and always wonder what could have been with Delaney." His jaw drew tight. "But I'll be damned if I'll just sit on the sidelines and give him a golden opportunity to take you away from me. So work out what you need to with him, but I'm going to be there every step of the way." His gaze shifted to Shane. "What do you say, man?"

Twenty

Max sat back on Summer's bed and relaxed. Middle Eastern music began to play, and he heard a clinking sound, then Summer flowed through the door in a trail of green veils and the delicate tinkling sound of beaded trim and coins. A glittery veil that flowed in color from a soft pastel green to a deep moss covered most of her body, but as she moved around the room to the music, she tugged the corner of the veil from her hip band, then unraveled it from her body. She swirled it around and around in a fluid movement that was stunning to behold.

The music slowed and she moved in front of him, her hips quivering in a rapid shimmy, her arms undulating at her sides. She was a dazzling sight in an intricately beaded bra that hugged her breasts and pushed them up at the same time. A beaded fringe hung from the bottom of the bra, lengthening to a V beneath each breast, caressing her stomach as her hips circled around in a figure eight. Her torso rotated in a seductive motion. Her hips flicked back and forth, sending the beaded hip band swaying. On her fingers, she wore small golden cymbals, which she clinked together in rhythm to the music.

The beat picked up again, and she spun around. Her full skirt twirled in a circle, swirling around her shapely legs. She moved around the room, her hips vibrating and her breasts swaying, beaded fringe rippling in a sensuous motion.

As the music slowed again, she sank to her knees, then eased backward until her head almost touched the floor. Her arms moved with grace, and she played the finger cymbals against the hardwood floor above her head, then snaked her arms in front of her again and brought herself upright. Gracefully, she eased herself to her feet and moved in a sensuous flow, her hips circling around and her shoulders shimmying, sending her breasts vibrating in a most arousing way.

Finally, the music stopped and she sank to her knees in front of him, her hands pressed together and her head bowed forward.

"Master, I am here to serve you. Command me."

His cock pulsed in desire. He wanted to push her back on the floor and drive his throbbing erection straight into her.

"Remove everything but your top." He wasn't sure how her costume came apart or whether the beaded hip band was part of the skirt or not, so he'd just leave the details to her.

She removed the waistband and laid it on the dresser, then shimmied out of the skirt, leaving it in a puddle on the floor. She turned around, and his gaze lingered on her shapely, naked behind as she pushed her tiny thong down her legs. She turned to face him again, and he grinned as he saw that she'd trimmed the usual neat triangle of her auburn pubic hair into the shape of a heart.

She removed a beaded necklace from her neck and metal arm cuffs, plus big hoop earrings and a beaded headband. He hadn't realized how many things she wore. Once she had removed the veil, what had held his attention had been her naked skin and the bra with the beaded trim that caressed her torso.

Now she stepped toward him, wearing only that bra. She knelt in front of him, then bowed down on the floor.

"Rise, slave."

She rose to her knees but kept her gaze downcast, playing the harem slave girl.

"You are very beautiful, and I have chosen you to share my bed this night."

"Yes, Master."

He cupped her chin and raised it until she gazed into his eyes.

"Kiss me."

She leaned forward and offered her lips. He met them and pressed his tongue between her lips. Her tongue met his, and they undulated in a dance of passion. He drew back and gazed at her. He ran his finger through the beads under her breasts and watched the glittery fringe sway back and forth.

"Delightful." He smiled. "Stand up."

She stood in front of him. He ran his fingers around her waist, then drew her closer. He pressed his face against the swell of her breasts above the bra, then kissed them. He dipped one finger under the fabric, stiff and heavy with the weight of the beads, and stroked her nipple. It jutted against his finger. He lapped his tongue under the fabric and curled around the hard nub. Then he moved to her other breast and did the same.

He shifted below her bra and pressed his lips between the curtain of beads and kissed her torso, then downward to her heart-shaped curls. He outlined the shape with his fingertip and chuckled.

"Lie down on the bed and open your legs."

She climbed onto the bed and stretched out, with her head on the pillow, and spread her legs wide. He kissed her ankles, then up her calves to her inner thighs. He licked and kissed the sensitive skin of one thigh, then moved to the other, then kissed up and over her hip, then to her belly, where he nuzzled her navel.

His hands stroked her inner thighs, then glided upward to her hot pussy. She gasped as he slid a finger inside, then kissed downward until he covered her clit with his mouth. He licked it while his fingers explored her hot inner passage. It dripped with need. He sucked on her clit, and she gasped and arched.

"You are wet and ready, my sweet. I think it's time you pay me a little attention."

He stretched out on the bed beside her, and she sat up. As she shifted toward him, he wrapped his hands around her hips.

"This way," he said as he drew her toward the top of the bed.

She climbed over him, her pussy directly over his face, then she grasped his cock and her lips glided over his cock head. He groaned at the exquisite feel of her hot mouth surrounding him.

He reached up and stroked her wet slit, gliding his finger forward and back. She sucked on his cock head as he slid his tongue into her.

Summer enjoyed the wonderful feel of his hot tongue gliding over her slit as she ran her tongue over his big cock head. It filled her mouth exquisitely. She sucked and squeezed him as her fingers tucked under his hard buttocks, then gasped as he sucked on her clit.

She opened wide and took him as deep as she could, stroking her hand lightly over his balls. She eased back, holding just his cock head in her mouth, and swirled her tongue around the underside of the corona. She tapped the tip of her tongue on the juncture on the underside of the shaft. He tensed under her and groaned against her clit.

He eased her around. "I want to be inside you. Now."

She turned around and crouched over him, pressing his big cock head to her slit. Slowly, she lowered herself onto his huge, thick cock. Feeling it push up into her. Stretching her. He wrapped his hands firmly around her waist, preventing her from gliding away.

"Now, show me some of those sexy dance moves again."

She smiled as she shifted her hip a little to the left, then to the right. Swaying back and forth made his cock pivot inside her. She moved her hips in a spiral, first clockwise, then counterclockwise. His cock swirled inside her, sending wild sensations fluttering through her. She alternately shimmied her hips and her shoulders, slowly at first, then picking up speed. His cock quivered inside her, and the beaded fringe swayed. His gaze fixed on her quivering breasts.

A second later, she felt herself flipped onto her back, and he prowled over her. His cock had slipped free, so now he pressed it against her, and with one quick thrust, she found herself filled again. He drew back, then thrust forward again.

She wrapped her arms around him as he thrust again and again.

Tingling pleasure jolted through her. Another thrust, and it pulsed within her. He tugged on the underside of her bra and pushed it upward, freeing her nipple, then he grasped it in his mouth and sucked mercilessly. She gasped, then arched her hips against him, allowing his cock to penetrate even deeper.

He thrust harder and faster, and she met every stroke, until pleasure exploded within her. She clung to him as she wailed in an intense orgasm. He joined her with a groan and an eruption of hot liquid.

They clung tight to each other as their heavy breathing subsided. He stared down at her single bare breast, her nipple pushing through the beaded fringe.

"That looks uncomfortable." He reached behind her and unfastened the bra, then removed it carefully, with a healthy respect for the finely detailed garment. He placed it carefully on the bedside table, then stroked over her bare breasts. He pressed them upward in his palms.

"I loved how these looked in that bra." He kissed one nipple, then the other. "But, I must admit, I like them this way even better."

Finally, he rolled onto his side and drew her against him, cuddling her close.

"Master," Summer said, "earlier, I noticed two men in the . . . tent next door."

Max stared at her. "Two men?"

A smile turned up his lips. "Those men are my friends,

and I want you to show them pleasure. Obey them just as you would me. Now go and fetch them."

Summer padded to the door, knowing Shane and Kyle waited in her den. She smiled at how quickly Max had accepted the idea. She had worried that he would need more coaxing, but apparently the belly dancing lessons she'd been taking for the past two years had worked their magic on him. She walked down the hall to the next door, then opened it, conscious of her nakedness. Kyle and Shane glanced up expectantly, then their hungry gazes devoured her.

She winked. "Coming?"

"I damn near did," Shane murmured.

The den was right next to her bedroom, with only a thin wall between the rooms, so they would have heard everything.

They stood up and followed her, striding into the bedroom behind her.

"Ah, my good friends," Max said, his arms opening in greeting. He pushed himself to his feet, mindless of his nudity, and sat in the chair beside her bed. "I am pleased you have chosen to take advantage of my hospitality." He gestured to Summer. "This is my slave, and she is ready to pleasure you. Order her to do anything you wish. She will obey."

Kyle dropped his pants and flung off his shirt. His stiff cock jutted forward. Summer wrapped her hand around his hard shaft and stroked as Shane divested himself of his clothes, too. Shane stepped forward, and she took his hard cock in her other hand.

"I want you to suck my cock," Kyle said.

She leaned forward and pressed her lips to the tip of his

cock and licked, then drew the head into her mouth. She licked and teased the tip with her tongue, swirling it around in circles as she stroked Shane's cock with her hand.

"I want you to suck both of us, back and forth," Shane said.

She released Kyle from her mouth and licked Shane, then took him inside. She bobbed up and down on him, then returned to Kyle. She bobbed up and down on one cock, then switched to the other. Three strokes, then she switched. Back and forth.

"I think our host should join us," Kyle said as she released him to move to Shane.

"If that is your wish." Max stood up and approached the bed, then stood beside Kyle.

Summer returned to Kyle, then shifted to Max next. She had to open wide to draw in his big, bulbous head, then she sucked it. She returned to Shane and sucked his head while licking under the corona. She sucked each of them several times, then bobbed up and down again. The men were getting stiffer and their bodies more tense. This time when she took Shane in her mouth, she stayed with him and sucked and licked until he groaned. She toyed with one of her breasts, and his breath caught, then he erupted in her mouth. She smiled and switched to Kyle, then sucked him until he, too, erupted in her mouth. Next, she dove down on Max's cock and squeezed him, then sucked and bobbed. A moment later, hot liquid filled her mouth again.

She lay back on the bed and cupped her breasts with her hands and stroked them. Shane and Kyle were already hard again, and Max was swelling. She opened her legs wide, aching to be filled by each of them.

"Do you want to fuck me?" she asked.

"I do." Shane climbed over her and pressed his cock head to her damp opening, then drove it into her. She moaned as his cock stroked inside her. He thrust, drew back, then thrust again. She was so close, she began to wail. His next thrust sent her flying over the edge.

"Oh, God, yes. I'm coming."

She clung to him as he drove into her again and again. She cried out in exquisite pleasure as he groaned his release.

She smiled up at Kyle, waiting for him to slide inside, but instead he sat on the edge of the bed and grabbed a tube from her side table, then slathered his cock with lubricant.

"Come over here," he said.

She knew exactly what he wanted. She stood in front of him, and he eased her back until his cock pressed against her back opening. She pressed against him, allowing his cock head to push into her . . . slowly, she pushed her inner muscles against him to allow him to push in deeper and deeper . . . until he was fully inside. He nuzzled her neck, then lifted her knees. Max stepped forward and drove his huge cock straight into her. She was so wet, he slid right in.

The intense sensation of Kyle's cock in her ass and Max's cock filling her vagina nearly made her come on the spot. Max moved slowly inside her. In and out, while Kyle glided inside her backside.

"Ohhhh . . ." Her moan turned to a wail as her body burst with electrifying pleasure and an orgasm engulfed her. Her entire body seemed to contract, then expand in a dizzying wave of bliss. Then full-out ecstasy. Kyle jerked in spasms behind her, and Max drove deep and hard, then filled her with his white hot release.

Summer turned to a boneless mass between them, enjoying the feel of their hard male bodies pressed against her. Max kissed her with passion while Kyle stroked her hair and nuzzled her neck.

Max finally drew back, his cock gliding free of her body.

Kyle helped her to her feet, then turned her in his arms and kissed her. As he drew back, he gazed at her, searching her face with somber green eyes.

As she gazed back at him, guilt simmered through her. Had she been wrong to draw him and Shane into this? Had she done irreparable damage to their continued relationship?

Kyle kissed her and nuzzled her ear. "It's okay," he murmured too quietly for the others to hear. "Everything will work out fine."

Kyle knew. Her worries . . . her fears . . . he read them in her face and knew what to say. Not that she'd stop worrying, but at least she knew she hadn't driven him away. And he'd talk to Shane.

Kyle brooded as Shane drove along the dark streets heading back to Kyle's house.

They had lost her. He knew it.

He thought that by joining Summer and Max, he could weaken the hold the man had on her. However, seeing Max's eyes as he'd made love to her . . . even with Kyle himself right behind her . . . inside her . . . He had been struck by the love shining in the other man's eyes.

Max loved Summer. And as much as Kyle wanted to ignore the fact, Summer was in love with Max, too. He knew her well enough to read her heart.

Kyle had no doubt he and Shane could develop a long, happy relationship with Summer, built on a strong foundation of trust, friendship, and caring . . . and that was a wonderful thing . . . but was that love the same as what she and Max had?

"Shane, about Summer . . . and Max . . ."

"Yeah, man, I know. And it stinks."

Twenty-one

Max opened the passenger door for Summer and noticed her hesitation.

"I want to take you somewhere special . . . and I want it to be a surprise," she said.

"Oh?" Max raised his eyebrows.

She pulled a black strip of cloth from her purse and held it up, clearly intending it as a blindfold.

"I'd like you to wear this," she said. "So I need to drive."

It was not proper for subs to make suggestions about where to go, to take the lead, and especially not to suggest her Dom wear a blindfold . . . but Max knew Summer didn't live the lifestyle. She wasn't aware of the rules.

"All right." He moved to the driver's door and opened it. Once she was comfortably settled inside, he closed the door and moved back to the passenger side.

He waited patiently while she tied the black cloth over his eyes, then as her delicate fingers played along the back of his head while she tied the knot. He felt her lean across him, then heard her pull the seat belt across his lap and click it into place. A moment later, the car engine started and the vehicle moved forward. He leaned back in the seat and enjoyed being chauffeured. The steady rhythm of the road lulled him, and a while later he realized he'd dozed off.

"How much longer?" he asked.

"Just another ten minutes or so," she answered.

A short time later, the car turned off the road and drove along a winding path, then stopped.

Summer opened his door and took his hand, then guided him from the car. He stepped carefully in the darkness of the blindfold as she led him forward.

"There are three steps here, going up," she said.

He pressed his foot forward until he felt the first step against his toes, then moved carefully up the steps, still holding Summer's hand.

"Watch the bottom of the door."

He continued forward, noticing the fresh breeze that had caressed his cheek had disappeared, then heard a door close behind him. The fresh outside air was replaced by the soft musky-floral scent of Summer.

"Good evening, Ms. Anderson," a woman said. "And welcome, M. My name is Sylvie."

M. That was how Tanya had referred to him in the acknowledgment in her book. He'd be willing to bet that wherever it was Summer was taking him, Tanya had suggested it.

"Ms. Anderson, this is Kara. She will take you to where you can prepare. I'll take M to your . . . room."

"Thank you, Sylvie." Summer leaned close to Max, and he could feel her soft breast brush his arm. "I'll see you shortly."

He heard footsteps, presumably Summer's and Kara's as they left.

"M, I'm going to take your arm and lead you down some stairs."

He felt her hand grip his forearm, and she guided him forward. She warned him of stairs, and once they'd reached the bottom of the curved staircase, she led him down a straight path. A heavy door closed behind them. Since someone had to close that door, he assumed someone else was here.

"Your woman has some interesting things planned for you, M. I'm going to prepare you."

Her fingers brushed his chest, and he realized she was unbuttoning his shirt. What the hell did Summer have in mind?

"I'm close to naked, M." Her voice purred seductively. "Don't worry, though. Your woman knows. After all, she did see me, even though you didn't. If you're a very good boy, I'll let you see before I leave." Her voice lilted in a teasing manner.

She finished undoing his shirt and tugged it from his shoulders.

"Well, someone works out regularly."

Her soft hand stroked over his stomach, then she eased him backward a half step until he felt padding against his back. Her fingers wrapped around his wrist and lifted his hand. Just as he was wondering if she was going to give him a feel of what were probably ripe, round breasts, he felt someone grab his free arm, too, and cold metal clamped around both his wrists.

What the hell?

Chains clanked as his wrists were pulled up over his head.

"We intend to leave you quite helpless, M."

As he felt her tug on his belt and release the buckle, he twisted his hands and found the chains above his wrists and grasped the cold metal links. As a hand slid his zipper down, he pulled his body up with his hands and kicked his legs upward, catching her between the legs and pushing her up against him. Soft and quite naked breasts bounced against his chest, and she grasped his shoulders, gasping in shock.

"I assure you, I'm anything but helpless," he growled. "If I order you to release my wrists, then you'll do it."

She was a sub, and as such, she would submit to his authoritative tone if he chose to command her. Also, this was a dungeon—he'd been to them before, though not to this particular one—and if he made it clear he did not intend to submit, she would be putting herself way out on a limb not to obey.

Slowly, he lowered his legs, and she stumbled to remain on her feet.

"So your lady is not a Domme, she is your sub?"

"Clearly, she has decided to turn the tables on me."

He could feel her heat as she leaned in close.

"If you would like me to help you teach her a lesson, I can arrange it." She stroked her hand over his chest. "You could teach me one, too. I will gladly accept your punishment."

"No, I will go along with Ms. Anderson's plans. The punishment later will be all the sweeter."

This woman lived the lifestyle—he could tell it wasn't just a job for her—so he decided to stay in the role. In fact, he was eager to see what Summer intended to do to him.

"May I have your permission, Mr. M, to remove your jeans?"

"Yes, Sylvie."

She released the snap, and his jeans fell away.

"And your briefs?"

He didn't know who was in the room helping her, but he had nothing to hide.

"Go ahead."

She drew down his briefs, and he smiled at her sharp intake of breath.

"My God, your sub is a lucky woman." Her fingers stroked down his belly . . . and lingered . . . then her hands slipped behind his head and she unfastened the blindfold, then drew it away.

Her short, glossy black hair was cut in a severe straight style with bangs. Her eyes were outlined in black, and her lips were glossed bright red. His gaze fell to her breasts—enormous, round mounds with hard rose nipples jutting forward. She wore black leather straps that surrounded her breasts and crisscrossed her slim torso, then continued underneath, widening just enough to cover her pussy.

"Mr. M, please remember I will gladly join your play if it would enhance your pleasure."

His gaze returned to her vivid blue eyes, which she quickly averted downward. He smiled.

"I'm sure it would, Sylvie, but I will leave that to Ms. Anderson."

He was pretty sure Summer wouldn't bring this other woman into it, but she was full of surprises tonight. Anything was possible.

Two bare-chested, muscular men dressed in leather pants stood behind Sylvie, and she gestured them away. They disappeared out a heavy oak door.

"I've been instructed to bind your ankles, Mr. M. And your waist."

"Go ahead."

She positioned his ankle where she wanted it, then fastened a leather band around it. She drew his other ankle sideways and fastened that one, too. He now stood with his feet shoulder width apart. Next, she fastened a wide, soft leather band around his waist, tightening it until it pulled him against the padded surface behind him.

"And, finally . . . your head."

He nodded. She fastened a strap around his forehead and fastened it to clasps on the padded surface behind him. Now his head was totally immobile.

Sylvie bowed her head, then stepped back.

"Your safe word is 'dog.' If you're gagged, blink rapidly five times."

She turned around, and her naked ass swayed seductively as she walked toward the door.

"Good-bye, Mr. M."

The large oak door creaked open, and Max watched Summer step into the dimly lit stone room. She wore a long, flowing black cape.

"I'll make this simple," she stated in an authoritative tone. "You enslaved my twin sister, so I have made you my captive. Now I will take my revenge. By the end of this night, you will call me Mistress."

Wonderful! Now that she'd given him the scenario, he knew exactly how to play the role.

He glared at her with a feral grin. "You mean you will call me Master . . . and plead with me to fuck you."

She blinked, clearly a little unnerved at his response, but she flicked her loose auburn hair over her shoulder and dropped her cape to the floor. Blood flooded to his groin at the sight of her in the erotic outfit she wore. Black leather straps with silver studs encircled her breasts with narrow straps radiating from them to hold a one-inch metal ring surrounding each nipple. Leather straps crossed downward over her navel to disappear between her legs to either side of her pussy, which was covered by a scrap of leather. Long fishnet stockings, the kind that stay up on their own somehow, stretched from midthigh down to her feet. She wore the black shoes with the slender metal heels he'd bought for her at the Sex-à-la-Gala show.

She perused his body and stared at his swelling cock.

"This monster needs to be on a leash." She wrapped a simple leather strap around his cock. The light brush of her fingers on him caused his cock to harden even more. She fastened the small buckle, but he continued to swell.

Damn, she doesn't realize it is getting too tight and she needs to leave some play.

He gritted his teeth but said nothing.

She glanced at it uncertainly. "Is it too tight?"

"If you're asking me to whine for you to release it, you're wasting your time," he growled.

His cock strained against the strap painfully. Her teeth tugged on her lower lip as she watched it, and she glanced up at him again. Finally, her fingers danced along the strap, and it pulled tighter as she released the buckle, then loosened. He held in his sigh of relief.

"I want you to be of use to me," she explained. "Thinking of you submitting to me has made me very wet."

She smiled as she stroked her fingers over her crotch, then she moved to his side and he felt himself rotating backward. The padded surface he'd been fastened to was a table that she could move into different positions with the flick of a control. Soon, he lay on the padded surface at an incline, his feet still near the floor and his head and shoulders about two feet off the ground.

She stepped over the table, placing her crotch in front of his face. She grabbed the fabric covering her pussy and tore it away.

She positioned herself over his mouth and lowered herself. Now her pussy brushed his face. With the straps around his head, he couldn't move his face if he wanted to.

He extended his tongue, and she glided across it.

"It feels so good having your mouth on me."

She moved back and forth over him. He watched her pussy undulate above him. His cock grew, and the sensual grip of the strap tightened around his shaft. He longed to drive the cock upward into her . . . hard. To hear her squeal in delight.

"Oh, I'm so close to coming." She ground her pelvis against his face, and he breathed in the erotic, musky scent of her as he flicked his tongue on her clit.

She rose quickly.

"You almost made me come."

She walked beside the table and stared at his naked torso. Then lower. A moment later, he felt her hand on his cock, then she bent down and her lips surrounded him. She sucked on his cock head . . . then licked his shaft, tracing her tongue around the leather strap . . . and, finally, his balls. Soon, he was rock hard.

She climbed over him and lowered herself onto his cock head, swallowing him into her opening. He savored that brief, hot pleasure . . . then it disappeared as she slipped away, torturing him. He almost groaned but kept a disciplined hold on himself.

"I want you to call me Mistress."

He simply stared at her.

"Call me Mistress," she commanded.

She looked incredibly sexy hovering over him, her breasts effectively naked with her nipples swollen in need.

At his silence, she lowered herself onto his cock head again, surrounding it with her heat, then she squeezed. It was exquisite torture.

"Call me Mistress," she demanded.

"No," he said.

She lowered herself a little more, drawing him deeper into her warmth, then she drew upward again, leaving his throbbing cock cold and twitching, only the very tip inside her.

"Do it," she commanded.

He held his silence.

She stroked his cock, and it ached with need.

Then she withdrew. She stroked her fingers into her slit, then stroked them over her nipples. They were hard and distended and all the more sexy with the cold metal rings surrounding them. He longed to take those fleshy beads into his mouth. The deep yearning must have shown in his eyes.

"Call me Mistress and I will squeeze you so hard inside me, you'll beg for release . . ." She grinned. "And then you'll get it."

Still he resisted, and she stroked her breasts, toying with those delicious-looking nipples.

Oh, God, he wanted her.

Her fingers slid over his cock, and he stifled a groan at the delightful sensation, then she grasped the strap and pulled it tight. He gasped as the leather bit into him . . . then it released and she tossed the strap aside.

She lowered herself onto his throbbing cock, taking him deep into her hot sheath, then she glided off, leaving his cock exposed to the cool air again. He wanted to be back inside her. She lowered herself and squeezed. This time, he could not suppress his groan. She slipped away again and stood up.

"Maybe I'll go rest for a while." She feigned a yawn, but he could tell she was as hot as he was. She started to step away, and he decided it was time to give her what she wanted.

"I will call you Mistress . . . if you'll fuck me right now. I want you to squeeze me with your cunt."

He'd used the C-word purposefully, to see what she'd do.

She raised an eyebrow. "I don't like that word. Call it something pretty."

He smiled. "Squeeze me with your pussy."

She crossed her arms in front of her and tapped her fingers. "I don't think so."

He grinned even wider.

"Mistress, please squeeze me with your beautiful, feminine passage of love."

Summer suppressed a smile. A little corny, but it would do.

"Call me Mistress and tell me you want me to fuck you. And do it nicely."

"Mistress, please fuck me. I need you so badly, I'll die without you. Mistress, I am your slave forever."

"That is nice. Especially that last part." She wished he really meant it, at least the forever part . . . but this was just a game.

She climbed over him and captured his cock inside her. His huge member stretched her and filled her so full, she wanted to cry out. She lifted and lowered, driving his monstrous cock deep inside her. She was so turned on that with the second thrust, she felt the waves of bliss claim her, and she wailed as an orgasm overtook her. She continued to bounce up and down, crying out in ecstasy as pleasure catapulted her to several orgasms one right after another. Beneath her, Max groaned, and she felt the force of his eruption deep inside her . . . which sent her pleasure even higher.

Summer awoke with a start . . . and glanced toward the door of the room. She felt . . . alone. She patted the bed behind her . . . and found it empty. She rolled over to see the hollow in the pillow where Max had been when she fell asleep in his arms last night.

After their very sexy role-playing in the dungeon, they'd moved to a bedroom in the inn upstairs and made love again in the comfort of the charming and homey room. He'd been passionate and loving and had held her close as they'd fallen asleep.

She pushed herself from the bed and wandered to the bathroom. Maybe he was having a shower. But the bathroom was empty. The only trace of Max was the lingering scent of his tangy aftershave.

She returned to the bedroom and glanced toward the

corner by the window where he'd left the overnight bag she'd tossed in the car for him yesterday. It was gone. Her heart sank.

Last night, she'd taken a risk and turned the tables on him, because she'd wanted to show him how strong she could be. Could her little adventure have driven him away?

It was at that moment . . . when she believed she had lost him forever . . . that she knew she'd fallen deeply and hopelessly in love with him.

The door lock clicked, and she glanced around.

Twenty-two

Summer saw Max standing in the doorway, and her heart soared.

"Good morning." He smiled. "I put my bag in the car and checked out. Would you like to grab some breakfast?"

Relief surged through her, along with joy at seeing him again and knowing she'd have a little longer with him before he left her life for good.

She nodded as she stood up and stepped toward him.

"Apparently, there's a great little diner around the corner," he said.

She slipped her arms around him and held him close, never wanting to let him go. He stroked her hair from her face and kissed her . . . sweet and tender. His charcoal eyes gazed into hers, dark and unreadable.

"You'd better get ready. They only serve breakfast for another hour."

"Yes, Master."

He wrapped his arm around her waist and drew her tighter to his body.

"I thought you were the Mistress now?"

She grabbed handfuls of his shirt below the collar and pulled his lips back to hers, then after a lingering kiss said, "I think you vanquished me in the end."

"No, I don't think anyone can vanquish you now that you've discovered how powerful you are. You can take on anyone and anything. There's no stopping Summer Anderson now."

He was smiling as he spoke, but Summer felt a sadness about him.

As they drove to the diner, mixed emotions tumbled through her. No matter what Max thought about last night, she shouldn't beat herself up about it. Right from the start, she'd known her relationship with him would be temporary. Even though he'd said he couldn't stop thinking about her. . . . They lived in very different places, leading totally different lifestyles. A big-city guy like Max would never move to a tiny place like Port Smith . . . and she would never be happy in a big city like New York. Surely he must realize that.

On top of that, she had Kyle and Shane to think about. Her relationship with them made more sense . . . well, as much as a relationship with one woman and two men could. And she loved them. Maybe not like she loved Max, but . . .

Her heart constricted at the realization. She loved Kyle and Shane . . . as very close and *intimate* friends . . . but *not like she loved Max*.

Max opened the car door for her, and she followed him into the quaint diner. She sat down in a comfy red booth facing him. She drank in the sight of him, wishing she could have happily-ever-after with him. Damn, why did life have to be so complicated?

Max ordered an omelet, and she asked for eggs Benedict. The waitress filled their coffee mugs. Once she'd gone, Max took Summer's hand and held it in the warmth of his.

"Summer, there's something I want to talk to you about."

She cringed inside. Was this it? The big good-bye?

"We've had a great time these past few weeks. And I've watched you grow. You've moved forward in your romantic life. You've shown incredible courage in establishing a very unconventional relationship with Shane and Kyle. You've grown past your fear of taking risks." He smiled. "I'd like to think I've helped you move forward."

So now he could move on. He was letting her down easy. Ending it on a positive note.

"Max, last night . . . when I dominated you . . ."

He sent her a half grin. "Yes?"

"Were you . . . okay with that?" she asked.

The intensity of his gaze burned through her.

"Okay? It was the highlight of our relationship." He nipped her fingertip. "You were sexy and bold and incredibly strong. To be honest, I've never trusted anyone else enough to play the sub role, but with you . . ."

The waitress arrived with their food, placing a steaming plate in front of each of them, then she topped up their coffee cups. When she left, Max pushed aside his plate and took Summer's hand again.

"Summer, what I'm really trying to say is, although you don't need me anymore . . . I need you. You've brought a joy to my life that has been missing for a long time."

Her breath caught, and she stared into his somber gray eyes and saw the vulnerability there.

"As you know, I loved once before," he continued. "I

had four blissfully happy years with my wife, Elena, and I believed no woman would ever replace her in my heart. As my feelings for you grew, I kept telling myself it wasn't love."

He tightened his hand around hers. "But when I thought about this ending between us . . . that I'd never see you again . . . I realized you had already insinuated yourself into my heart. . . ."

She stared at him, not willing to believe where his words seemed to be leading.

"Max, what are you trying to say?"

He kissed the back of her hand, the tender brush of his lips sending a quiver through her.

"I'm trying to tell you . . . I'm in love with you."

The blood froze in her veins. She couldn't be hearing him right. It didn't make sense.

"But you live in New York. How will we . . . ?"

He shrugged. "I can do my work from Port Smith. I don't need the city."

He stood up and pulled something from his pocket, then knelt down beside her. Her heart swelled as he opened a small, blue velvet box and flashed a huge diamond ring that glittered in the morning sunlight.

"Summer, will you marry me?"

Twenty-three

Summer's lips turned up in a smile that was almost painful in its intensity. She could feel the gaze of every patron in the restaurant on her.

"I . . . uh . . ."

Her heart swelled in joy. Oh, God, she loved Max so much.

"Yes." Tears filled her eyes, and she dashed them away. She threw her arms around him. "I love you, too, Max. Of course I'll marry you."

The room erupted in applause.

Max had suggested she wait a few days to tell Kyle and Shane so they could enjoy a little pre-honeymoon before facing the real world again. She'd arranged a few days off work, taking a short trip to New York with Max. But now that she was back, she was dreading her first encounter with Shane or Kyle. How would she break it to them that she was engaged to Max?

Summer heard a car pull up in her driveway, then a door close. She hurried to the living room, worried it was one of them. She gave a sigh of relief when Max stepped inside, holding a gift-wrapped box. Crimson wrapping paper tied with a wide gold ribbon and a huge bow.

A tingle ran down her spine. She loved surprises . . . especially from Max.

She set the package on the coffee table and slid the ribbon off the side of the box, then removed the lid. She pulled back the red tissue and found . . . chains. She lifted them out of the box and realized they were connected, attached to a black leather collar. A leather thong with a chain attached vertically along the front sat in the tissue, along with an envelope. She opened it and pulled out a postcard with a picture that showed a model wearing an outfit of leather and chains.

Ah, that's what this should look like. Black leather surrounded the lovely blonde's neck, and the chains cascaded below her breasts, while the leather thong hugged her lower body.

She glanced at Max, then smiled. She unbuttoned her blouse, slowly and purposefully, then slid it off her shoulders and dropped it on the couch. Next, she unzipped her skirt and shimmied it over her hips, then let it fall to the floor. She stroked her hand up her thigh seductively. Encouraged by Max's heated gaze, she hooked her fingers under the elastic waistband of her thong and tugged it outward a little . . . then allowed it to snap back into place. She grinned and scooped up the box, then walked with a purposeful wiggle to the bedroom.

Let him wait for it.

She stripped out of her underwear and referred to the picture as she attached the black band around her neck. Three chains dropped from the collar and connected to other chains to surround her breasts and drape underneath in an elegant cascade. It was a little like her belly dance bra, but with no actual bra. It was more like a harness of chains. She pulled on the leather thong and realized the chain that ran along the crotch actually covered an opening.

She glanced at herself in the mirror. Wow. Her breasts were totally naked, and her pubic area, although fully covered, was fully accessible.

She felt sexy and . . . wicked.

Glancing in the box again, she realized there was something else inside, lying diagonally across the bottom. Long and black, with a touch of glitter. She lifted it out and realized it was a riding crop. She hadn't known such a thing could be so lovely, with a gorgeous black leather handle adorned with sparkling crystals. A narrow leather wrist strap attached to the handle, and the other end had a short leather strap. The shaft was plaited with black leather to give an elegant textured look. She pushed her hand through the wrist strap of the riding crop and smiled.

She pulled open the bedroom door and sauntered into the living room, then stared at Max and lightly slapped the riding crop against her palm.

Max grinned broadly, his charcoal eyes simmering with heat.

Summer struck a sexy pose with her hand on one hip, riding crop jutting to the side at an angle, and her other hand behind her head, pushing her hair forward in a mass of waves over her shoulder. His gaze wandered her body, sending a thrumming heat through her.

In his hand, he held a square gift box. It was wrapped in

the same red gift wrap, with a gold bow but no ribbon. She lifted off the top and peered inside. Nestled in the red tissue was a black leather collar.

She glanced back to Max in time to see him thrust open the coat he wore—which was an odd choice for a warm summer evening—then drop it on the floor.

"Oh, my."

He looked godlike in black leather briefs, studded along the edge with silver, and studded straps encircling his torso. She longed to press her hand against his well-defined abs and stroke over those broad, muscular shoulders of his.

He stepped forward and knelt before her. He lifted his chin, and she realized he was inviting her to attach the collar. She placed the box on the coffee table and lifted the collar from inside, then curved it around his neck and attached the buckle at the back.

"Thank you, Mistress." He took her left hand and kissed the diamond ring.

She ran her fingertips over the pointed studs on his collar, then slipped her finger through the large metal ring at center front and tugged upward.

"Stand up," she commanded.

He stood up and bowed his head. "I will submit to your will, Mistress, but first—if you would allow—I have another gift."

She grinned. "By all means. Bring it in."

Max stood up and strode to the front door.

Was he going to go out to the car in that outfit? She wondered what the neighbors would make of that.

He pulled open the door.

"Wow. That is sensational on you," Shane said from the doorway. Kyle stood beside him.

Shock careened through her. Oh, God, she had to tell them about her and Max . . . but . . . not dressed like this . . . with Max dressed as her slave.

"What are you doing here?" she asked.

It barely registered that they both wore coats, too, and carried boxes just like the second one Max had given her. They both shrugged off the coats they were wearing, and her eyes widened. They also wore black leather briefs, Shane's with chain adornments across the front, Kyle's with a zipper along the crotch. Black leather straps crisscrossed their bodies, accentuating their sculpted chests and abs.

"I know how Mistress enjoys a harem," Max said.

So Max had invited them over to play. Did he think it would make it easier for her to tell them about their engagement after sexual play? Her heart clenched. How could she tell them in the afterglow of sex, all snuggled up in bed with them?

Kyle and Shane both stepped forward, then handed her the boxes they held. As she opened the first gift box, to find a leather collar with a short chain across the front, along with the silver ring, both men knelt in front of her. Shane offered his neck as Max had done.

She attached his collar. The second box held a plain collar with just the silver ring and no adornment, which she attached around Kyle's neck. Shane took her hand, and she almost tugged it away as she realized he was going to kiss it.

He's going to see the diamond ring.

She held her breath as Shane's lips lowered to her hand and . . . kissed the ring. No surprise showed in his sky blue eyes. Her eyes widened. Kyle took her hand and kissed her ring, then winked at her.

"Oh, my God. You knew!"

"Yes, Mistress," Shane said. "Max explained to us that he will be your husband, but he invited us to be your loyal servants, too."

"And"—her gaze strayed to Kyle—"this is okay with you?"

Kyle met her gaze. "Summer, we love you, but we realize now that it's a love between friends. Very *close* friends who share a deep respect. It isn't the same as what you feel for Max. And what he feels for you."

Her shaking hand rested on his cheek. "I can't believe how wonderful you're both being about this. I was so afraid I'd hurt you."

"We want what's best for you, Summer," Shane said. "Always."

She blinked back a tear. "So . . . how will this work?"

Max stepped forward. "We know it's a highly unconventional arrangement, but . . . you and I will be married, and Shane or Kyle, or both, can join us whenever we all agree. Of course, they'll be free to date other women."

Her heart thundered in her chest. They wanted to have a relationship . . . all four of them?

How lucky could a girl get?

She nodded, filled with wonder at this unusual proposal. "And when they find another partner, of course, this will end."

"Unless you don't mind another woman joining our group," Shane said with a wink.

Well, the future certainly promised more intriguing situations!

Summer grinned, then sucked in a breath as she stared at the three of them in front of her, Shane and Kyle still kneeling.

"Slave Max, come here."

He stepped toward her.

"I want you to kiss me with exuberance and passion. . . ."

He wrapped his arms around her. "My pleasure, Mistress." His gaze locked on hers with a searing heat, accompanied by an undeniable softness.

His lips claimed hers as his strong arms drew her close, and she melted against him.

She wanted to say, *Take me, Max. Make me know I'm yours.* She wanted him to press her down on the bed and take her to heaven.

But that would come. Now was the time to celebrate the beginning of the relationship with all four of them . . . together.

His lips parted from hers, and he drew back. With the riding crop, she gestured for him to kneel again, and he obeyed.

She walked around behind them and noticed that their briefs were actually thongs, as her gaze lingered over three sets of hard, muscular buttocks.

She paced back and forth behind them, gripping the jeweled handle of the riding crop and tapping the other end against her palm.

"Before I make a decision, I'll have to see how well behaved you are . . ."

She flicked the riding crop against Kyle's behind. It smacked against his flesh, leaving a glowing red mark. Next, Shane received the end of her crop, then Max. Not one of the men flinched, and now each wore a red mark of distinction . . . her brand of approval.

". . . and how well you play together."

She stood with her feet apart and her hands on her hips.

"Slave Kyle, get over here and lick me."

On his knees, he shifted toward her and pressed his face to her pussy. He drew the chain aside, and his hot tongue pushed through the slit in the leather, then pressed between her slick flesh and licked. His tongue delved into her again, sending her pulse racing.

"That's enough. Now Slave Shane."

Still on his knees, Kyle moved to the side as Shane moved toward her. He licked her hot slit, his tongue flickering from side to side, then he teased her clit. Her knees felt weak. More of this and she'd tumble to the floor.

"Stop."

She sat on the couch and bent her knees, placing her feet on the edge of the cushion, leaving her pussy totally exposed to their view.

"Slave Max, come over here and lick me. You have three minutes to make me come."

Max moved to the edge of the couch, and his mouth covered her. His tongue dipped deep into her, then assaulted her clit with purpose. He sucked, then squeezed her sensitive bud in his mouth. Her fingers raked through his hair as his raging assault pushed her pleasure higher and higher. Suddenly, she wanted more than his tongue.

"Fuck me, Max. Right now."

At her words, urgent and ragged, he grabbed her hips and drew her to the edge of the upholstered seat, then he tugged his briefs below his cock and pushed it against her. In one forward thrust, he impaled her. Before he'd finished two strokes, she wailed in orgasm. Still he thrust, again and again, as she clung to him, wrapping her legs tightly around him. The intensity of the pleasure surged through her as his cock pounded deep and hard within her.

Finally, he slowed, holding her close against his body. His cock was still rock hard.

"You haven't come," she murmured as he withdrew.

"Mistress did not give me permission."

She grinned, amazed he'd been able to hold back.

"That is true." She stood up and walked toward the bedroom. "All of you follow me." She pointed to the armchair at the end of the bed. "Slave Max, sit there." She glanced toward Shane. "Slave Shane, come here."

As he stood in front of her, a good head taller, as all the men were, she quivered in anticipation. She hooked her finger under the top edge of his briefs, at the hips, and tugged.

"Take these off."

He disposed of them instantly.

"Now sit down in the chair."

Shane sat down, and she dragged the tip of the riding crop along the shaft of his swollen cock.

"Very nice."

She retrieved a tube of lubricant from her bedside table and tossed it to him.

"I want you to put that cock of yours in my ass," she commanded. "But first . . ." She tugged on the waistband of her own thong. "Take these off."

She stood in front of him. He slid his fingers under the

top edge of the small garment and drew it downward . . . over her hips . . . down her thighs . . . then to the floor. She stepped out of them, now naked except for the cascading chains and leather neck band she wore, which covered nothing.

Shane opened the tube and applied the gel. She turned around, and as she lowered herself, he placed his cock head against her back opening. Slowly, she eased downward, taking him a little at a time. He stretched her as he pushed deeper.

Finally, she sat on his lap, full of his cock, and leaned back against him.

"Stroke my breasts, Slave Shane." Her voice was low and seductive.

He cupped her breasts in his big, strong hands and stroked. Her nipples puckered, aching in need.

"Slave Kyle, come over here."

He knelt in front of her.

"Suck my nipples."

Shane released one breast to allow Kyle to take her nipple in his mouth and stroke it with his tongue, then he drew it deep into his mouth. She sighed in pleasure. A moment later, he switched to the other nipple, and Shane took her wet-tipped breast in his hand again. Feeling the two men touching her . . . stroking her . . . sent her pulse rocketing.

"Oh, yes. That's lovely." In fact, she could barely catch her breath. "Now stuff that big cock of yours in my pussy." She almost said "cunt," just to feel like a bad-ass Domme, but she couldn't quite do it. "Pussy" still fit the bill for talking dirty as far as she was concerned.

Kyle dropped his briefs, pressed his cock to her lower lips, then pushed inside. Slowly. Damn, it felt good having his cock glide into her. She wrapped her arms around him as he filled her to the hilt.

It was heaven being sandwiched between these two big, muscular men, with their hard cocks filling her. With her third man across the room, his gaze glued to them.

"Max, are you watching?" She knew he was. She could see him in the mirror.

"Yes, Mistress."

"Stroke your cock while you watch."

He pushed down the leather briefs and dropped them to his ankles, then kicked them away as his hand wrapped around his huge cock.

Would he be able to stop from coming while the two men fucked her, especially while he was stroking his cock in time?

"Kyle and Shane, fuck me."

Kyle drew back, then drove his cock deep into her, and she gasped. Shane lifted his pelvis, pushing his cock deeper. They found a rhythm, and soon her heart pounded in her chest as the two cocks thrust into her repeatedly.

"Oh, yes." She clung to Kyle's shoulders as both cocks drove deep and pulled back. Again and again. "Oh, God, I'm going to . . ." She sucked in air as pleasure pulsed through her. "Come. I'm . . . coming."

Intense bliss shot through her, carrying her to heaven. The two men pumped and pumped, and she remembered . . . "Kyle . . . come."

At the feel of his eruption inside her, she wailed in release again.

Somehow, Shane held on. Their pumping decreased and finally came to a stop.

"Kyle. That was very good. Now sit and watch."

She glanced at Max as his hand moved up and down his still fully erect cock.

"Max, come over here and fuck me."

Max surged across the room and filled her before she could catch her breath.

"Fuck me. Both of you fuck me like you mean it. And I want you both to come."

Between Max's huge cock in front and Shane's in back, she felt impossibly full.

Max drove deep, then pulled back, then drove deep again. At the same time, Shane pulsed up and down. It was too much. She wailed in ecstatic bliss. Both men erupted at the same time, and she shrieked at the increasing intensity of her orgasm. Every nerve ending exploded with sheer, potent pleasure. As the men pumped into her, she felt her body float into an impossible realm of pure ecstasy.

Everything faded away to a mindless, numbing pleasure.

"Summer?"

She felt someone patting her cheek.

"Summer, are you all right?"

She opened her eyes to see Max staring down at her, concern lining his features. Her lips curled up on a smile.

"Oh, I'm much better than all right. I'm absolutely divine."

"I'll second that," Shane said behind her, his cock still embedded inside her.

Max's too. She wiggled a little, feeling them move inside her.

"Mmm. What a lovely sensation."

She sighed. They could certainly follow her commands, but could they play together without her being in charge all the time?

"You are all very strong, virile men, and I think you don't want to stay under my power. I think you can find a way to overpower me and make me your prisoner."

Max surged forward, driving his cock, which had stiffened at her suggestion, deep into her again. She gasped in pleasure and fell back against Shane's strong chest. Shane's hands glided down her arms, then he grasped her wrists and held them behind her. Max pumped into her a couple more times, then withdrew.

Kyle stepped forward and slipped his stiff cock into her and rode a few times. When he withdrew, she felt herself lifted from the chair. Kyle threw her over his shoulder and carried her to the bed.

Max appeared with a rope and began coiling it around her legs. Soon, Kyle and Shane were inside her, front and back, thrusting, as she sucked Max's big cock in her mouth.

All three men were inside her.

An hour later, wrapped in Max's strong arms, Kyle and Shane stretched out beside them, she sighed. Life didn't get any better than this!

Read on for a preview of Opal Carew's
upcoming erotic romance

Forbidden Heat

available from St. Martin's Griffin in Winter 2010

Danielle Rayne wheeled her suitcase into the elevator and
turned around. As the doors were closing her gaze caught
on two tall, attractive men, one with sandy blond hair and
one with light brown hair, neatly tied back in a ponytail.
They were crossing the hotel lobby toward the reception
desk, both stylishly dressed in slim fit jeans.

Oh, my God. Jake and Trey.

The two men she had fantasized about for almost fifteen
years. Two men who had haunted her dreams. Kissing her.
Holding her. Her cheeks flushed as hot, sweaty images from
those dreams rippled through her mind.

The older woman standing beside her glanced her way.

"Are you okay?" she asked, kindly blue eyes taking in
Danielle's burning crimson cheeks.

"Yes, fine, thank you. Just a bit of a cold coming on,"
she lied.

She took a deep breath and tried to steady her racing
heart. As much as she yearned to be with Jake . . . or Trey . . .
or both . . . it would never be. Because Jake and Trey were in
love . . . with each other.

At least, they used to be. When she knew them in college.

Were they still together? They had arrived at the hotel together. Of course, that wasn't such a surprise. A lot of the old gang would be here. Danielle had flown to Buffalo to attend her old friend Harmony's wedding.

Old friend? Well, more like an acquaintance now. She and Harmony could have had a close friendship, but Danielle hadn't kept in touch, even though Harmony had tried for a while. She'd sent e-mails, Christmas cards, letters.

Danielle had always intended to write her back, but never seemed to get around to it. Eventually Harmony's e-mails and cards tapered off, and then stopped completely.

Danielle didn't mean to sabotage her chances at friendship, but somehow, by inattentiveness, she always seemed to manage it. She knew that she had issues with letting people get close, but a part of her desperately wanted closer relationships with people. Wanted a friend to share things with, a friend to talk to, someone who cared about her.

The elevator doors opened on the fifteenth floor. She smiled at the lady beside her and stepped from the elevator, then pulled her suitcase behind her down the long hallway toward her room.

"You're in room 1512, Mr. Jamieson. I hope you enjoy your stay."

Trey glanced at the lovely desk clerk's nametag, then returned her smile with an added wink.

"Thank you, Georgia."

Her cheeks flushed slightly.

Jake nudged his friend's arm as they stepped away from the desk.

"Stop flirting with the poor woman," Jake said with a grin. "You know it's not going to go anywhere."

"Why do you think that?" Trey asked as they approached the elevator.

"Well, for one reason, because we're meeting with Nikki and Angela tonight."

Trey pushed the elevator call button. "Sure, but then there's tomorrow."

He glanced across the lobby at the lovely blond Georgia as she consulted her computer. She swept her long waves of silky hair back over her shoulder, then glanced up to see his gaze directed at her. She smiled luminously and then returned her gaze to her current client, but Trey could tell the woman was interested. Very interested.

"And who knows . . . maybe Georgia would be interested in joining us tonight."

Jake chuckled. The elevator doors whooshed open and he followed Trey inside.

"What? Two women not enough for you?"

"Well, I do have to share with you . . . and I don't think Nikki or Angela would mind."

"No, I'm sure they wouldn't."

The doors opened and Jake exited the elevator, followed by Trey.

"Down this way," Jake said as he headed left down the hallway. "I think they're the two at the end of the hall."

Danielle unzipped the vinyl cover and removed the aqua dress she intended to wear to the wedding tomorrow, then hung it in the closet. She heard male voices in the hall and peered out the peephole. Jake and Trey walked by her room.

Good heavens, they were on the same floor! In fact, since she was the second to last room from the end, they must be in the room next to hers, or the one across the hall from that one.

They were definitely still together, Danielle decided. They'd arrived together and now it seemed they were in the same room. She heard a door open, then click closed.

Although she wished the men were free and single . . . *and liked women* . . . it made her heart swell to think that their relationship could last so long. She hadn't experienced much of that . . . relationships that lasted. Nothing in her life had been stable and the thought that someone else could make a go of a relationship . . . could actually find another person to depend on . . . to love . . . and who loved them back . . . it made her feel a little better about the world.

As Danielle watched Trey cross the lobby, she decided to say hello. He entered the lounge off the lobby and she followed him, hurrying to catch up. She stepped into the dimly lit room and glanced around. Trey walked toward a woman with long flowing blond hair standing at the bar. Danielle slowed as he slid his arm around the other woman's waist and leaned toward her ear.

"Hey, sweetheart. Waiting for someone?"

She turned and smiled at him, then wrapped her arms around him in a more than friendly embrace. In fact, she plastered her exceptional body against his in a frankly suggestive manner.

"Only for you, Trey." She nipped his earlobe.

Danielle sucked in a breath and turned to leave, shock swirling through her. Trey interested in a woman? What about Jake? Or was Danielle wrong and they weren't still together?

She hurried from the bar.

Jake entered the lounge and saw Trey and Angela sitting and laughing at a table in the corner. When Angela saw Jake approach the table, she stood up and gave him a big, warm hug.

"How you doing, sexy?" she asked. "I've missed you."

"And yet it's only been five months. Not like our usual year."

He and Trey met with Angela, Nikki, Cole, and Harmony once a year—all old friends from college—for a week of wild, no-holds-barred sex. The Group of Six had been meeting for over ten years now and, it seemed, would now be the Group of Seven, since Harmony had met Aiden and was now getting married, bringing Aiden into the fold.

Trey stood up, too.

"Nikki just called to say her plane was late so she's just gotten into her room," Angie told Jake. "She suggested we go to the restaurant and get a table and she'll meet us there."

Jake hooked arms with Angie and Trey took her other arm. They stepped outside into the warm evening.

"I'll get us a cab," Jake said.

"Actually, the place is just a block down, so we can walk," Angie said.

He glanced at her three-inch spike heels, accentuating the shape and length of her lovely legs. "In those heels? You sure?"

"Oh, honey, you know I can do anything in a pair of high-heeled shoes."

Jake's cock swelled as he remembered some of the things

she had done, wearing only a pair of spike heels. The woman was intensely creative.

They entered the classy Italian restaurant.

"Please, follow me," the moustached host said as he led them through a maze of hallways passing small groupings of tables in intimate niches along the way. "Is this to your liking?" he asked when he stopped at a booth in a niche of its own.

"Lovely. Thank you." Angela slid into the booth. Trey slipped in on one side of her and Jake on the other.

"Our friend told us to be sure and try your house wine, so please bring a carafe and four glasses," Trey said.

"Right away." The man hurried away.

Trey smiled at Angela. "Harmony raved about this place."

Jake felt Angela's hand glide along his thigh, and he was pretty sure she was doing the same to Trey.

"Well, I certainly like the atmosphere."

Jake slid his hand along her silky thigh, then slid beneath her dress. He glided upward along her soft skin, then his fingers came in contact with her soft blond curls. She wore no panties. He slipped inside her silken folds. She was already wet.

Angela did love being naughty, as she called it, in public.

He leaned in and kissed her ear. "You like that, sweetheart?"

Her eyelids half closed as he stroked over her clit. "Oh, you know it."

Jake felt Trey's fingers join his inside Angela. His gaze caught Trey's and he grinned. Angela leaned back against the seat and sighed as Trey stroked inside her and Jake quivered his fingertip over her clit.

"Oh, you guys know . . . ohhh . . . just what I like."

She moaned softly, a sound easily hidden from other diners by the soft dinner music playing in the background.

Her hand tightened around Jake's thigh and she sucked in deep breaths. A second later, she moaned in earnest, as she climaxed under their touch.

He loved watching her come. She enjoyed sex so much and in such an easy manner. This woman had no hang-ups. Just a pure love of sex.

"Hey, what are you three up to back here?"

Jake glanced around at the mock scolding voice.

Nikki held her face in a frown, then giggled, unable to hold the stern expression any longer.

"I see you started without me."

"Don't worry, honey," Angela said as she straightened in her seat. "They're still very interested." Her hand glided over the firm bulge in Jake's pants. "Believe me."

"Let me see." She slid in beside Jake and stroked over his cock, too. "Lovely."

She kissed his cheek and smiled at Trey.

The waiter arrived with a glass carafe of red wine and four stemmed glasses. He filled the glasses, then handed them each a menu.

"Maybe give us fifteen minutes or so to decide," Nikki said to him with a smile.

"Very good, miss." He hurried away again.

"Do you think it will take you that long to decide on a meal?" Trey asked, one eyebrow cocked.

"Not at all," Nikki said. "It's just that I already know what I want for an appetizer."

She slipped downward, disappearing under the table. Jake felt her hands on his belt.

Angela also slipped under the table.

A second later, he felt his zipper slide down and Nikki's soft fingers wrapped around his aching cock. She stroked up and down, and his semi-erect cock swelled to rock-hard rigidity. Her warm lips wrapped around him and he moaned as she drew him into her warm mouth. She glided up and down on his hard cock, sending pleasure rippling through him. She sucked, then squeezed. She drew him impossibly deep into her mouth, covering him in her intense heat . . . and sucked hard . . . and stroked his balls.

He couldn't hold it. He erupted in her moist, welcoming warmth.

A moment later, she slipped back into her seat, then licked her lips before she took a sip of wine. She had a way of making a man feel that she totally loved pleasuring him. He glanced toward Trey just as he reached his own climax. His facial features tightened and he groaned softly, obviously in intense pleasure, Angela clearly working her magic on him. She reappeared a moment later, settling in between Trey and Jake.

These were two amazing women. If only he could find someone in his regular life who could make him feel as special as these two women could. And Harmony, too, but she'd found her significant other. A man she loved and with whom she would spend her life.

Jake glanced at Trey, smiling as Angela whispered something in his ear. Of course, Jake had also found the man *he* loved but, unfortunately, that man wasn't ready to commit to another man. And probably never would. Jake had figured that out long ago and had let go of that type of relationship between them, settling for friendship. Even though a part of him still yearned to make it work.

After dinner, the four of them returned to Trey's room. Trey opened the door and gestured them inside.

As soon as he closed the door, Nikki wrapped her arms around him and pressed her soft lips to his. Her tongue slid inside his mouth and she stroked his tongue. He slid his tongue the length of hers, undulating in an erotic dance.

"Trey, I am so hot right now."

She slipped away from him and tugged the zipper down on her dress. Of course, she would be. She'd come late to their play session in the restaurant and was the only one who had not been pleasured.

She dropped her dress to the floor, leaving her standing in only a turquoise bra with matching garter belt and stockings. No panties.

"Well, let me help you out."

He drew her into his arms and kissed her deeply, then reached around behind her and unfastened her bra. As she slipped the cups of the bra from her ample breasts, he reached forward and stroked her soft mounds. The nipples protruded. He captured one in his mouth and sucked lightly. She moaned. He scooped her up and carried her to the nearest bed. Angela stripped off her dress and bra as she watched Trey lean down and suck on Nikki's other nipple. Jake shed his clothes as the two of them settled on the other bed, watching Trey stroke over Nikki's ribs as he licked and sucked first one nipple, then the other.

Trey stood up and shed his clothes. Angela's hand

wrapped around Jake's long, slender cock and stroked up and down. Trey stroked Nikki's thighs and eased them open, then leaned forward to dip his finger into her slick pussy. His tongue slid along her hot, moist flesh, then pressed against her rigid button. She moaned as she grasped his head. He flicked his tongue against her, easing off when he could tell she was close, then flicking rapidly again, unrelenting. He sucked on her clit, then dabbed lightly. Finally, he prowled upward. She immediately grasped his aching cock and stroked it, then pressed her hand on his chest and pushed him backward until he lay on his back. She climbed over him and pressed his cockhead against her hot, wet opening . . . then eased down on him, swallowing him into her hungry sheath.

He groaned at the exquisite heat.

She squeezed him, bringing him close.

She leaned forward to kiss him.

"That is such an inviting angle," Jake said while Angela continued stroking his rigid cock.

"Well, accept the invitation, sweetie," Nikki said with a wink.

He kissed Angela, then stood up and grabbed the tube of lubricant from the bedside table. A few seconds later, he climbed on the bed behind Nikki. Trey watched the look of rapture on her face as Jake pressed his slick cock into her ass.

"Oh, you two are so . . . oh, God . . . it feels so incredible when you both . . ."

Jake pressed forward. Trey pushed deeper into Nikki. She moaned.

There was something incredible about sharing a woman with Jake. About knowing his own cock was deep inside

Nikki at the same time as Jake's was. Trey thrust into Nikki and she moaned. He thrust again, immensely turned on by Nikki's pleasure, and the heat around him . . . and knowing Jake's cock was almost touching his as they both thrust into her.

"Oh, yes. That's incredible." Nikki moaned. "Fuck me. I'm . . . Oh, yeah . . . I'm coming."

She wailed, long and hard. Trey erupted in a searing burst of pleasure.

Danielle lay in her bed, trying not to listen to the moans of pleasure in the room next to hers. A woman wailed loudly.

Danielle had heard the four of them pass her room a little while ago. She'd glanced out to see Trey and Jake with two women, then heard someone enter Trey's room. She assumed Jake took the other woman to his room across the hall.

As hard as she tried, she could not stop listening to Trey and his woman friend.

Finally the woman stopped and Danielle sighed in relief. Maybe now she could fall asleep. Except visions of Trey making love to the beautiful blond woman she'd seen him with earlier haunted her. Her nipples, needy from the erotic sounds, stood bead-hard. She stroked them, knowing this would not help her fall asleep.

A few moments later, she heard a woman moan again.

So soon?

Actually, it was not just one woman. She heard two women now. She listened more closely. And two male voices.

My God, they're both in there. And with two women.

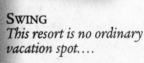